STAY ALIVE

THE JOURNAL OF DOUGLAS ALLEN DEEDS, THE DONNER PARTY EXPEDITION, 1846

BY RODMAN PHILBRICK

D0064608

SCHOLASTIC INC.

This book was originally published by Scholastic Inc. in 2001 as part of the Dear America: My Name Is America series.

While the events described and some of the characters in this book may be based on actual historical events and real people, Douglas Allen Deeds is a fictional character, created by the author, and his journal and its epilogue are works of fiction.

Copyright © 2001 by Rodman Philbrick

❖ ❖ ❖

All rights reserved. Published by Scholastic Inc., *Publishers since 1920*. SCHOLASTIC and associated logos are trademarks and/or registered trademarks of Scholastic Inc.

No part of this publication may be reproduced, or stored in a retrieval system, or transmitted in any form or by any means, electronic, mechanical, photocopying, recording, or otherwise, without written permission of the publisher. For information regarding permission, write to Scholastic Inc., Attention: Permissions Department, 557 Broadway, New York, New York 10012.

The publisher does not have any control over and does not assume any responsibility for author or third-party websites or their content.

ISBN 978-1-338-71908-6

❖ ❖ ❖

10 9 8 7 6 5 4 3 2 1   21 22 23 24 25

Book design by Elizabeth B. Parisi
Photo research by Zoe Moffitt and Arlete Shaeffer
Printed in the U.S.A.   40
This edition first printing, 2021

For my brothers, Philip, Jonathan, and Mark

✦ ✦ ✦

What happened to the Donner Party Expedition during those brutal winter months in 1846 and 1847 is a horror almost beyond description. Almost. Douglas Allen Deeds kept a journal of these awful events, down to the last gruesome detail.

Read if you dare.

✦ ✦ ✦

1
THE WAY WEST

May 12, 1846
Independence, Missouri

"Today I embark on a great journey."

That's what Mr. George Donner told me to write down when I bought me a vellum-bound journal from the stationery store but I didn't know what to say.

"The first sentence is always the hardest," Mr. Donner said. "The rest is up to you."

Thank you, Mr. Donner, for thinking up that first sentence, and for letting me tag along on your wagon train even tho I ain't got no kin and no wagon, but only poor old Barny, who don't want to leave Missouri if he can help it.

Barny is my horse, which I got when my paw passed. The horse and one hundred dollars in gold from selling the farm, that's all I have in the world, but it's enough to get me there, if I'm careful.

Last thing I did before leaving Independence was pay my respects to Maw and Paw. I went to the little churchyard with all the pretty white markers and prayed over 'em and explained how before long my prayers would be coming from California. Maw didn't know about California, she's been gone so long, but Paw did. Before he died, he talked about how there were valleys where it never snowed and crops that grow all year long. California is where a man can eat a fresh peach in December and never be cold, Paw said. Which is probably what gave me the idea to join up.

May 13

Our expedition is big and getting bigger. Two hundred wagons and more every day! When folks hear where we're headed, they sell their land for ten cents on the dollar and buy a wagon and follow along. George Donner and his brother, Jacob, organized the train in Springfield along with Mr. James Reed and Colonel Russell. Mr. Donner says he don't mind all the extra folks. He says there's safety in numbers and plenty of food along the way. All the game we can hunt and good water for the horses.

Ho! For California!

May 14

We are already two long, hard days from Independence, but have made less than ten miles progress. Mr. Reed says a few more days and we'll be clear of these dense, dark timberlands and out in the open plains where the going will be easier. I asked him how many times he's led settlers through to California, and he gave me a funny look, like I was trying to be insulting, which I wasn't. I have the greatest respect for Mr. Reed and the Donner brothers, even if none of them has never actually been west before. Paw always said there's first time for everything!

I made a new friend today. His name is Edward Breen. His family has three wagons and twelve good horses. The way Edward's mother dotes on him reminds me how much I still miss my own maw, even tho I was but five years old when she passed. I am fifteen now, so I pulled my hat brim down so nobody'd see me cryin'. I felt considerable better afterwards when Mrs. Breen insisted I hitch up with them, and eat with them and so on. She's a real nice lady, and I like the soft way she talks, which I suppose is how everybody from Ireland talks.

There's a number of other young single men in the party, and mostly they stick together. Some of the bachelors drink hard liquor, which I made a vow never to touch, so I'm glad of the kind invitation to accompany the Breens.

While we were walking along, guiding the teams of oxen that pull the wagons, I entertained my new friend, Edward, by recounting all the Missouri whoppers I could recall (they work better if you give them a honey-mouth drawl). He laughed so hard he spit water through his nose! He especially liked the one about the catfish that swallowed the bear.

Edward says when we get to California maybe me and him can partner up and be surveyors. He says with all the free land being cut out by new settlers there'll be a shortage of surveyors, marking out the property lines and so on, and we'll prosper. He was so excited about the idea I didn't tell him I've got my heart set on farming dairy cows, which is what my paw tried to do until he had his run of bad luck.

Nobody has ever seen anything like the Donner

expedition. It is two miles from the first wagon to the last, and the ground shakes as we go by. We make such a racket it sounds like every pot and pan in the world is falling downstairs at the same time. All us men helped cutting trail today, and at first the track was firm and the wheels didn't sink. But by the time the last wagon passed, the trail weren't nothing but soggy mud, and we had to set down straw and pry the wheels clear. It is hard work, but I don't mind. Everybody is so friendly and grateful for our common purpose.

Mrs. Tamsen Donner saw me scribbling in this journal and said to be sure to put in some stuff about rations, so here goes. We got a ration of a hundred and fifty pounds of flour and seventy-five pounds of salted meat per person. You got to buy that much, or you can't join up. Seventy-five pounds of meat won't last for such a long journey, but we expect to hunt game on the way. We got rice and beans and lard for frying. Every wagon has at least one spare wheel and the fixings to make more. Each family has a tent and gear for cooking, and many have spare horses. Most every man has a rifle, and mostly they're pretty handy, even if they never shot anything but rabbit and squirrel.

That won't matter, as we expect to find buffalo near the Platte River, and they say buffalo are a mighty big target and hard to miss. I never ate buffalo steak and am looking forward to it.

May 15

We are free of the forests! This morning, three hours after dawn, we came at last to the end of the timberlands, and saw the sun rising clear over the great prairie. In Missouri I never seen anything so wide open to the sky. Just fields of tall grass as far as a man can see. No, I lie, much farther than a man can see. More like what an angel might see, looking down from Heaven.

Mr. George Donner says if all goes well it will take no more than two months to traverse the prairie lands and that, come August, we'll cross over the Sierra Nevada mountains and find ourselves in California.

Right off, things have improved considerable. Colonel Russell, who is helping to lead the party, rode ahead to spot for Indians. He didn't find any, but he did locate a fine hard trail that is in such splendid condition it can almost be called a proper road. No more wheels bogging down in the mud! By Mr. Donner's reckoning we made better than ten miles in a single day and should expect to do even better tomorrow.

I shot a pheasant and Mrs. Breen praised me so, I'm sure it made my face as pink as bunting. She says the Breens will never go hungry so long as I'm there to help provide, and she hopes I'll teach Edward to shoot as good as me. I didn't have the courage to tell her the pheasant just happened to light on a tree stump so close by nobody could have missed. Anyhow, Mrs. Breen made up a batch of fine biscuits and gravy, and that pheasant sure tasted good!

Later Mr. Patrick Breen (Edward's paw) made a fuss over putting a pheasant feather in the brim of my hat. He don't say much but when he does, it means something. I count my lucky stars to have such friends.

No buffalo yet, but birds and small game are plentiful.

May 16

Mr. James Reed kindly invited me to admire his Palace today. I never seen anything like it. The Pioneer Palace Car ain't no ordinary wagon. It's so big it takes four yoke of oxen to pull it. The Palace has got a real door and steps to get up, and inside it's all fitted out like a little house on wheels, with a woodstove to keep it warm, and a stovepipe that goes up through the canvas top. They got built-in beds below, and a loft where the children sleep, and a special feather bed for their grandma, who is ailing. She don't complain, but just lies in her bed and sighs a little. They even got a library in there, with a bunch of books!

Their daughter's name is Virginia. She's twelve years old and has a pony called Billy. When she saw me scribbling in my journal, she told me she was keeping one, too. Hers will be better, I guess, 'cause she's had more learning than me, and books to read and stuff.

The way they talk, I get the impression the Reeds don't think much of the Donner family. The Donners got three wagons, but none of them compare to the Pioneer Palace Car, that's for sure.

Just before sundown I tried for a deer, but missed, and it ran off.

May 17

After two hours on the trail we came to the Kaw River, and got ourselves across it, and on into the frontier territory, leaving Missouri behind.

Turns out the Kaw Tribe own this patch of river, and if you want to cross over, you got to pay them. That's the deal, and Mr. James Reed said it was pretty fair, considering. We got 247 wagons in our party, and it cost a dollar each wagon, so the Kaw made a pile today. Mr. Breen joked how the Indians were getting even for selling Manhattan so cheap. I asked what Manhattan was, and he said it meant the same as New York, which is somewhere back east.

Anyhow, them Kaw worked mighty hard for the trade. What happens when you want to cross their river is this: First you pull the wagon as close to the landing as you can get it, then you unhitch the teams of oxen, which will be unyoked and then swum over. Then the Indians take charge. Each wagon gets shoved onto the landing, and from there gets manhandled onto their rickety little barge, which is a tricky business. The barge barely has room for two wagons. Once they get the wagons on board, the Indians pole the barge to the landing on the opposite shore, and then do it all over again, only backward, unloading the wagons onto the landing and then shoving them up to the shore.

They had to make a special trip for Mr. Reed's Pioneer Palace Car because it's so much bigger than a regular wagon, but they still only charged him a dollar.

Meantime, we're all busy swimming the oxen across the river. They don't like it much, but if you push hard enough, they go. And once an ox gets going forward he won't back up. Horses mostly go better. We didn't lose one animal, which Mr. Reed says is a triumph.

Naturally I got soaked to the skin, but you know what? It felt good. I ain't been so clean of dust since we left Independence!

We were all proud of ourselves about the crossing and slapped each other on the back and said we were sturdy pioneers and how nothing could stop us now. Then Mr. Donner came by, real somber and serious-like, and said that at the next river we cross there wouldn't be Indians to help us, and no barge to float the wagons. Mr. Reed didn't say anything, but he wasn't pleased.

We got a mile clear of the landing, and then made camp. Patrick Breen has a fiddle and played it very lively after supper. Everybody sung along, even if we didn't know the words, and we all felt mighty fine about deciding to go west.

Later, when it came time to bed down, Mrs. Breen said I should sleep under their wagon, in case it rained. Edward elected to sleep outside, too, so's I could tell him some more Missouri whoppers. He's holding the lantern while I write in my journal and says "Hello."

May 19

For the last two days we been following the Kaw River. The land is flat and easy, tho it bogs down some here and there. Me and Edward take charge of encouraging the oxen while his father and the others push and shove the wagon from behind, rocking it free of the mud.

The work is hard, but nobody complains much. Mr. Breen jokes a lot and says how all of Ireland is nothing but a bog. You can tell he misses Ireland, even if he won't admit it, because he's an American now, bound for California. It don't matter where you came from because you can't go back. You can only keep going. We got that in common with the oxen!

May 20

Rain. Bad rain. Terrible thunder and wicked lightning, too. It started about noon, but we kept going for three hours, trying to make a few more miles. At last it was too much. The lightning scared the horses, so we all stopped and made camp, which today means we huddle inside the wagons, feeling scared and miserable. When the lightning goes off, you can see it flashing right through the canvas top, bright as the sun. The lightning casts a shadow, too, tho it don't last long.

Mrs. Breen weeps a little, because she's afraid we'll be struck, and her husband comforts her as best he can. They talk real soft to each other, which reminds me of my dear maw and paw, God rest their souls.

The Breens are very kind to have me in their wagon, as by rights I should be outside with the other bachelors. The wagons are up on a plateau, some distance from the river, and pretty exposed to the wretched weather. Our whole wagon shakes whenever a gust hits us. The canvas top had some waterproofing, supposedly, but it ain't holding, and we're all wet and miserable as dogs.

Edward jokes that I look like a muskrat with a pen, and I guess he ain't far wrong.

May 29

Virginia Reed's grandmother died today.

I mentioned before how she mostly just lay on her feather bed and didn't say much, on account of the sickness in her lungs. Mr. Reed says it was the stopping that did her in. As long as the wagons were moving west, her condition improved, but we been stopped the last few days, and that's what failed her.

We been waiting for the Big Blue River to go down enough to cross over. It's flooded high from all the rain, and if it don't drop, we'll have to fell trees and make rafts to get the wagons across. Meantime, we had a proper funeral for the poor old woman. I asked why she came along if she was feeling poorly, and they told me she couldn't bear to be apart from her family, because of fear she'd never see them again. I guess the old woman didn't want to die alone, and she didn't.

Anyhow, the funeral was a fine thing. Naturally, we don't have any coffins along, so we chopped down a cottonwood tree, and some of the men hewed it into planks and made a coffin. The whole party followed the coffin to a big oak tree, and a hole was dug in a shady spot, and the coffin laid inside. The Reverend Cornwall read from the Bible, and it gave the family some comfort to know that their blessed grandmother was now in Heaven, and would help the Lord watch over us, and keep us safe until we reached our destination. Then another one of the men found a suitable stone and carved her name in, and the day she was born and the day she died. We all dragged the stone to the grave, and then little Virginia planted wildflowers around it.

"She was the best grandma in the whole world," says

Virginia, kind of fierce. "She told me stories and gave me all the hugs I wanted. I'll surely miss her."

Then she dried her tears. I think she's very brave for a girl.

May 30

All day we been felling trees and building rafts for the wagons. The stronger men handled the big felling axes while me and Edward and a bunch of the others chopped off the branches, once the trees were down. Then we yoked up teams of oxen and drug the logs near the river. The Big Blue River is still flooded with rainwater and looks like it'll never fall, which is why we got to raft across it if ever we're to get where we're going.

To make the rafts, we roll the logs together and rope them up tight, but the wagons being too heavy, they'll have to be emptied before they can be floated across. Once we get them across, each wagon will have to be reloaded and packed. Mr. Reed expects it'll take us two more days, just ferrying wagons and goods to the other side.

It sure is a lot of hard work, trekking to California!

Mr. Donner and his whole family work hard, without complaint, and do their best to ignore the sharp comments Mr. James Reed makes about how things will go faster and more efficient if someone is elected leader of the expedition, meaning him. He always seems to know what to do and isn't afraid to say so.

This evening, after a late supper, and with folks too tired for singing, Virginia invited me and Edward to see The Book.

"This is what got Father started," she told us. "Once he read The Book, we had to sell everything, and have the wagons built, and raise an expedition. He knew he could do it, you see, because of what The Book said."

She opened The Book and showed us the title page. It looked very grand. *The Emigrants' Guide to Oregon and California*, by Lansford W. Hastings. She wouldn't let us touch it, in case our hands was dirty (they were, a bit) but we studied that title page, and a few others throughout, and were mighty impressed.

Virginia told us Mr. Hastings has thought of everything. He tells all about the wonders of California and exactly how to get there: the best routes across the prairie and through the mountain passes, and what equipment and supplies we need, and how to travel and deal with unfriendly Indians, and so on. She said he thought of everything, and then he put it in his book.

Edward and I allowed that we were grateful to Mr. Hastings for writing such a marvelous book, and to Virginia for letting us see it.

Then her father came in. One thing you can say about

Mr. James Reed, he fills up whatever space he's in. At first he seemed sort of mad we were studying his book, but when he saw we had the proper respect for the thing, he give us a fine lecture, probably as good as anything in The Book.

"You began this great journey as boys, but by the time we arrive at our destination in the rich valleys of California, you will both be men. We must expect a certain amount of hardship along the way, and many difficulties, but with Mr. Hastings as our guide, we'll make it. We must cleave to his knowledge and his inspiration. He has discovered a new shortcut, and if we follow his directions, and the trails he has marked, we'll save ourselves 350 miles, and be settled in our new homes before the snow flies."

Then Mr. Reed told how he intended to have himself appointed overseer of all the Indian nations west of the Rocky Mountains, on account of his connections to a certain politician in Illinois by the name of Abe Lincoln. He puts a lot of stock in this Lincoln, almost as much as he does in Lansford Hastings, even tho Lincoln never wrote no book about pioneering.

"Say good night to your friends, Virginia. Tomorrow will be a long day."

Me and Edward then left, and I wrote all this stuff down before I forgot it, especially the part about The Book.

June 3

The Reed family tied a black flag on the Pioneer Palace Car, to mark the passing of their grandma. I notice Virginia don't sit in the big wagon much, but prefers to ride her pony. It is a splendid little pony, and very lively. Me and Edward, mostly we walk alongside the oxen, making them go. You might say we're walking all the way to California. Twelve miles a day ain't much, tho. Back in Missouri, many's the time I walked twenty miles or more, going to town and back.

We're passing through mighty rough country, and most of our time is spent freeing up wagons and such. This one time an ox that belongs to Mr. Jacob Donner got stuck in a ditch and couldn't back out. Me and Edward joined with the others to heave it out. The poor ox rolled its eyes and bawled, but it was fine and dandy once we got it free. Folks always say "dumb as an ox," and that animal might be dumb, but Mr. Donner says mostly it was scared because it didn't know what would happen next—like us human folk when the thunder starts booming.

Later in the day there was a bad accident. The German wagon tipped over and broke. We call it the German wagon because the owner, Mr. Lewis Keseberg, is always shouting and swearing in that language. Most times he's in foul temper, and today he had good reason. A wheel came loose from the axle, and the whole wagon tipped over sudden.

Mrs. Keseberg got shot right out of her seat and ended

up in a deep puddle. She had her baby in her arms, and both of them got soaked to the skin. Mr. Keseberg then set out cursing his wife like it was her fault the wagon tipped over, and he might have hit her if Mr. Reed didn't threaten to beat him within an inch of his life.

Mr. Reed balled his hands into fists and shouted that if Keseberg dared strike any woman on this wagon train—any woman, especially his poor wife—he vowed to lay his fists upon him and pummel him.

"Do you understand me, sir?" Mr. Reed roared.

Mr. Keseberg stared at him real sullen, but backed off and let his wife get to her feet.

Mr. Reed then told him if he wanted to strike something, he should strike that wheel back on the axle, and stop acting like a d—mn fool.

Mr. Keseberg then said there weren't no cause for swearing, which is pretty funny, considering. Anyhow, it did make him leave off cursing at his poor wife for a time, tho after supper I heard her crying inside their busted wagon.

Mr. Reed heard it, too, and gave that wagon such a look I'm surprised it didn't burst into flames.

June 5

We are camped on the Little Blue River. I am plumb weary, as we made twenty miles today, and twenty miles of driving oxen feels like walking fifty miles. Yes, I am tired, but it sure feels good. If we keep up like this, we'll make California in no time.

Yesterday I shot me an antelope. And I was the only one in the whole party to do so!

What happened is me and Edward elected to ride out ahead when the wagons stopped at noon, taking our bacon 'n biscuits with us. My old horse, Barny, seemed glad to get away from the dust and chew on some fresh grass.

We weren't gone but a mile before we spotted the critters.

"Look there," said Edward, real low. "Deer."

But I knew immediate they weren't deer. They were colored different and had sharp curvy horns, not antlers. Also they didn't move like deer, but leaped and bounced like they had springs on their hooves.

I told him they must be what they call antelope and that I intended to get us one for supper.

I got down from Barny, slipped the rifle out of the saddle holster, and made signs to Edward that we'd have to advance without the horses. We crept up through the long prairie grass, blind as beetles, figuring if we couldn't see them, they couldn't see us. Every now and then I'd glimpse the top of a horn as they bounded along.

Luckily we were downwind when we spotted them, so they didn't sniff us out right away. I figured the critters didn't have much experience with people, or being hunted, and I was right. Because when I popped up out of the tall grass, the herd sort of froze for just a heartbeat, and that gave me time to get off a shot and drop the biggest antelope. It was dead before it hit the ground, with my bullet through its heart.

They are such pretty critters it makes you feel sad to have killed one. But I didn't feel sad for too long, the way they fussed over me back at the wagon train. We had that antelope for supper, shared out with the whole party, and it tasted good and warmed our bellies. Everybody remarked that antelope tastes like venison, only better. Mr. Breen has kept the horns and hung them on his wagon in my honor.

Mr. George Donner said it was a lucky day when I joined up, and even Mr. Reed said what a good shot I was, even tho he don't much like to give credit.

I must stop here, before I fall asleep. Yesterday, an antelope. Today, twenty miles! I'm mighty glad I decided to join up, and only wish my maw and paw were with me.

Maybe they are watching over me. I pray so.

June 8

At last we have reached the Platte River. The valley is ten miles wide, with great bluffs on either side, and the peaceful river right in the middle. The land on either side is firm, with no trees, and forms a natural highway for our wagons.

When we came up over the last bluff and first saw the beautiful valley before us, Mr. George Donner raised his hand. "Behold," he said. "Yonder is our earthly Paradise. Follow the valley road and we shall come to Heaven."

By Heaven he means California. He said the Platte is famous among the westbound emigrants, for it will take us all the way to Chimney Rock, deep in the Indian Territories. Most everybody going this way passes along the Platte, and there's already a trail worn down by the wagons that come before. All we have to do is follow it, and we can't go wrong.

The river is near a mile wide but shallow enough to wade across. Looked for fish but didn't see any. Mrs. Tamsen Donner is busy writing down the names of all the wildflowers that grow along the river. Some are bluer than the sky, and others so yellow it makes your eyes hurt, and some as red as drops of blood. Everywhere there is sage that smells like lavender.

We are in Pawnee country, but so far we haven't seen any Indians. All day we trekked along the river, which has many low islands, big and small. If we weren't so occupied with keeping the oxen going, I'd have me a swim in that river and maybe build a raft to float out to the islands, to explore and so on. But there ain't time for nothing but going forward and making up for all the days we lost bogged down. No matter. It feels good to be moving, and everybody is cheerful.

We are passing a great long island that splits the Platte River into two forks. Colonel Russell, who was scouting ahead, says the island is fifty miles long! Sometimes the Pawnee make camp on the island, but there was no sign of them today. We did come across considerable buffalo bones. They are bleached white by the sun and stick up out of the soil. There were so many we could have filled every wagon full of those bones if we wanted. Seems like this place must have been a hunting ground once upon a time.

The other thing there's plenty of is buffalo chips, which burn even better than dried cow chips. Which kind of makes sense, since buffalo don't eat nothing but grass and sage. Anyhow, there ain't much dried wood around, so once you get a fire going you just pile on a few buffalo chips and the fire will glow hot and steady. Don't smell that bad neither, considering. Mr. Breen says it's like burning peat back in Ireland, only cheaper.

I asked if they have buffalo in Ireland, and he laughed and said no. We ain't actually seen any live buffalo yet, but expect to any day now.

Meantime, we have found messages left for us written on buffalo skulls and stuck up on poles beside the road. The messages are from settlers who have gone on ahead, letting us know what to expect. Some had trouble with Indians, others got bogged down in the mud. We are most fortunate and don't have trouble from neither Pawnee nor rain. I got me one of them buffalo skulls and wrote on it: *smooth sailing* and signed my name, *Douglas A. Deeds*. I figure that will cheer up whoever finds it, to know that our party has passed through with no trouble.

Later

Tonight me and Edward sat up late, after the fires had smoldered down to glowing ash. We looked up at the stars and out across the river, where the islands blended into the mist.

Edward said it was such beautiful country that maybe we should all stop and settle. Him and me could build us a fort out on the big island.

I agreed it was pretty, but reminded him it was summer, and that the winters were harder here than back in Missouri. We must keep on to California, I said, for that is our true destination.

Edward asked if I thought we'd make it.

I had no doubt, I told him, and neither should he.

Then I told him a pretty good whopper about the Missouri bullfrog that bought himself a suit of clothes and ran for office, and got elected, too.

Edward soon fell asleep, but I sat up until late, looking

at the stars and writing in this journal by the last glow of the fire.

June 13

Today is a rest day. We have made such good progress along the Platte Valley, and it has been so dry that many of the wheel rims have come loose. Part of resetting a wheel means holding it over a fire to heat the iron rims, so the whole camp smells of fire and smoke. I don't mind. It gives me a chance to catch up on my journal, which has been neglected these last five days.

Much has happened. An eight-year-old boy died, and Mr. Reed shot an elk. The boy I didn't know. He got run over by a wagon a few weeks back and died of infection. We all mourned him, of course, like we mourned Virginia Reed's grandmother. They say at the end the boy didn't even complain but just drifted off to Heaven. Probably they're saying that to make us all feel better, but I don't mind. On the day the boy got buried, a woman from another wagon gave birth to a baby that lived, and we all took that as a good sign.

Before the elk got shot or the boy passed, we came upon some trappers. They were a scurvy bunch, with long filthy beards and black teeth. They had fur and skins to trade for flour and coffee and whiskey, and some did so. The trappers acted friendly, but I didn't trust them none.

I seen hard men like that in Missouri and they'll lie to cheat you, just for the sport of it. Once they got what they wanted, they went on their way and was seen no more.

Edward Breen and me were out for elk, too, having seen them in the distance, but Mr. James Reed got there first and brought one down. He was mighty pleased with himself, but shared the elk out with the whole party. It was a sizeable animal, near as big as a horse and fed many—more than my poor little antelope!

June 15

Buffalo!

The word came back from a scout that a vast herd was sighted. Me and Edward saddled our horses and went out. Three miles from the wagon train we came to a high bluff, and once we gained the top, we saw them down below us. At first I thought it was a forest of dark brown bushes, there were so many, and then I could see them moving real slow. Buffalo grazing the prairie, all the way to the horizon.

Edward said he had never seen so many of one thing, and that there must be thousands.

All I knew was, there were too many to count. We were still so far away they looked small and delicate, but when you get closer, buffalo are bigger than cattle, with great furry coats and thick curved horns.

I told Edward we mustn't scare them. Scare them and they'd stampede, and we didn't want no part of a buffalo stampede. I advised as how we should sneak up until we got in range. Then once they sensed us, we'd ride full speed straight at them and pick out our targets.

Edward looked at me as if I'd lost my wits. "Have you lost your head?" he asked. "You just said we mustn't let them stampede!"

He had me there. I tried to explain it was different if the stampede was running away from you, but Edward kept shaking his head and wanted to know how I knew they'd run away from us instead of at us. He thought maybe we should leave the whole operation to more experienced hunters.

That riled me. I told him there weren't no experienced buffalo hunters in our party, and the only way to get "experience" was to go ahead and do the thing and see what happened.

Edward said we could get killed. I told him we could get struck by lightning, too. Or run over by a wagon like that poor boy. You worry on things like that, I said, you're in the wrong business.

I meant the dangerous business of being an emigrant to California, and Edward understood. He sighed and patted his horse and agreed to my plan.

We walked the horses a mile or so, stopping to let them

graze, so the buffalo might think we was part of the herd. I'm no expert, but I know this much: Buffalo ain't scared of horses, because horses are smaller than buffalo. Buffalo are like any other wild animal. They get scared by what they don't know, and a man on a horse riding at them full speed, firing a rifle, that'd scare anybody. So the idea was to get as close as we could by moving natural, and not giving them a reason to fear us.

We got to within 100 yards before the big bulls started sniffing and snorting and wondering what was wrong about us.

"Get yourself ready," I whispered, slowly putting my hand on the horn of my saddle. "Now!"

I leaped on my horse and charged straight at the buffalo herd. Edward was right behind me. The big bull buffalo tried to get the herd running, but we was too quick. We got so close you couldn't miss. I picked out a sizeable buffalo and fired. The poor critter didn't know what hit it. Edward got one, too, and he ain't much of a shot.

By then the whole herd was running hard, heading for the far horizon. It sounded like a thunderstorm rumbling under the earth. The dust from their hooves got so thick we could barely see. After it settled down, I told Edward to ride back and get a wagon while I stood guard over our two buffalo.

Later in the day, five or six other men were also

successful, and we all returned in triumph to the camp and were welcomed like heroes.

We'll be eating steak all the way to California!

June 23

Today we reached Chimney Rock. Mr. Donner says it is the Eighth Wonder of the World. It could be, because I ain't never seen nothing like it before. We could see it for miles and miles, how it stood like a beacon to guide us, and it lifted our spirits to know we had made some progress.

We finally arrived about noon, and each of the families set up to prepare its midday meal. Some made fires, and others ate what was cold—there are those who like cold beans, but I ain't one of them.

Edward stayed with his family, and I went off to explore. The base of the Wonder is a hard, sloping rock, and on top of the rock is the famous Chimney, which is only about fifty feet wide but soars 500 feet straight up. Stand under it and look up at the sky, and it'll make you dizzy, guaranteed. Nobody knows how it got there, whether it was carved by wind or water, or by the hand of God.

I studied the Chimney for a good long while, then come back to the wagon and ate. We are still feasting on buffalo. There were biscuits, too, but the flour is getting short.

June 25

Much has happened in the last few days. We crossed over the South Platte River, and right away the country changed. Now it is more like desert, with tumbleweeds and a few cactus trees and not much fodder for the oxen and cattle. We are deep in the Indian Territories that some folks call Nebraska, tho we still ain't come upon the tribes that live here.

Our group has shrunk considerable, too. We had 250 wagons once, but are now down to less than fifty wagons, because so many have quit or gone off on their own, or hitched up with other parties.

I heard Mr. Breen tell his wife he is worried about our progress. He says we are at least 200 miles behind schedule, if we hope to make California by September. Then his wife shushed him and said not to speak so in front of the children, and that all would be well once we reached Fort Laramie.

June 26

Indians!

Today we came upon several bands of Sioux. They have pitched their tepee tents nearby a trading post. Many more lodges of Sioux are expected, for they are getting ready for a war with the Crow. The Sioux warriors are finely dressed in buckskin and wear many handsome ornaments made of shells and bones. They are friendly to emigrants passing through, tho Mr. Reed says they would not be so polite if we tried to settle within their territory.

One of the younger braves kindly let me see his scalps, which he had taken in a previous battle with his Crow enemies. The scalps don't look like much, but I praised them, and he was mighty pleased. We didn't have no words in common but understood each other just fine. I suppose he is not much older than me, but already a warrior that has proved himself, and very proud.

A lot of the folks left letters at the trading post, to be taken back East. I wrote instead in my journal, which is sort of like a letter posted to myself, to read when I am older.

June 27

Today we met a real mountain man. He was dressed all in buckskin the color of dirt, and his long beard was dusty and gray. He said he had been traveling with Mr. Lansford Hastings, the man who wrote the *The Emigrants' Guide* that Mr. Reed and Mr. Donner value so highly. Except the old mountain man wasn't so impressed as they were.

The mountain man said Hastings was a fool and didn't know any more about taking a wagon train of emigrants through the mountains than he does about riding a moonbeam.

Mr. Reed give him a look and asked if he was jesting. The mountain man said crossing the Sierra Nevada range was a hard go. He said it was one thing for a man on horseback to cross over, but an ox-drawn wagon presented another problem entire. He said Mr. Hastings didn't know his way around and had no experience. He said all Hastings has got is a load of untested, unproven, high-flown ideas that he's passed on to innocent folks like us.

"Sir, I think it is you who are the fool," said Mr. Reed, his eyes flashing.

"Think what you like," said the mountain man, "but I know the mountains and Hastings don't, and that's a fact. I have come to warn you not to trust either his maps or his advice. You would do better to follow the rest of the parties who are already well ahead of you. Follow in the ruts their wagons make, and don't deviate from their path, and you might just make it."

I could tell from the set of his jaw that Mr. Reed wasn't listening to the mountain man. He had already made up his mind that Mr. Hastings was right, and he didn't want to hear different.

The mountain man said that winter comes fast, and if we got stuck and run out of food, maybe we could eat Mr. Hastings's book. And with that, the ornery fellow turned on his heel and showed us his back.

"Pay that fool no heed," said Mr. Reed sternly. He then lectured us all on the superior wisdom of following Mr.

Hastings' directions, and told us the mountain man didn't want us crossing the lands where he trapped, because he was afraid we'd hunt his game and steal his furs.

Mr. Reed said it was nothing but raw greed that motivated the mountain man. That is why he tried to frighten us off. As to Mr. Hastings' qualifications, consider this: He has published a guidebook and the mountain man has not. Who should we believe, an ignorant trapper or a man of letters?

I expect Mr. Reed is right. The mountain man looked honest enough, but his type are crafty people and very jealous of their hunting grounds.

We continue on our way, with Mr. Hastings' book as our guide.

July 4

Today is Independence Day, and we all celebrated in grand style.

This morning we were roused at dawn by a bugle and rose to see a newly sewn flag flying from a pole on Mr. Reed's wagon. The flag has twenty-eight stars, and Mr. Reed predicted that someday soon a twenty-ninth star would be added, and that would be California. We all cheered, and many rifles were fired into the air, startling the horses.

We are encamped with several other wagon trains that

are resting for the holiday. Some are heading to California by various routes, others to the Oregon Territories, but we all have one thing in common. High hopes. High hopes that we get where we're going in one piece, and then strike it rich!

That's what old Colonel Russell said when he stood up on a stump and made a speech. "Friends! Countrymen! Lend me your ears! That means listen up, 'cause I got a few words to say on this joyous occasion! It has been seventy years since the United States of America was born and it ain't stopped growing yet, and there is room enough for everybody, and free land for the taking!"

Colonel Russell had to shout to make himself heard, but then again, he's a man who likes to shout. He did go on and on, remarking on just about every single thing that had happened in the last seventy years, and telling us what he thought about it, and why we should all agree with him.

Edward's father finally shook his head and said, "Give a man a stump to stand on, and a crowd to shout at, and he will flap his jaw."

Me and Edward then crept behind the stump and lit some firecrackers that he had saved special for the occasion. When the firecrackers went off, everybody applauded because they thought it meant Colonel Russell's speech was finally over. It wasn't. Finally they stopped him by offering him a glass of whiskey, which he said was better than lemonade.

After supper everybody from all the wagon trains gathered together and sang and danced. Edward's father took a turn at the fiddle and then danced a jig with Edward's mother, who laughed so hard she got a pain in her ribs and had to stop dancing.

Later, when the children were sleeping, some of the men told jokes so raw I don't dare write them down, or the page will burn.

Tomorrow we will make necessary repairs and rest the oxen one more day.

July 6

This morning I saw a most marvelous thing. Hundreds of Sioux warriors stood at attention by the side of the trail as our wagons passed. It was an awesome sight. Each had a flower in his mouth, which is a sign that they wish us a safe journey. Later the younger braves got into high spirits, galloping their ponies through the wagon train, whooping and hollering.

"They're excited about the coming war with the Crow," Mr. George Donner told us. "No doubt many of them will die in battle. Right now they are trying to fill themselves with courage, to overcome their fears."

Mr. James Reed overheard him and muttered

something about Donner not knowing his rear end from his elbow, and how would he know what the Indians were thinking? But in my opinion, Mr. Donner got it right. A man don't march to war where he might get killed without first working himself up to it.

Anyhow, we almost had a bad incident that might have turned ugly except for the Sioux chief. It happened like this: Some of the younger braves took a shine to little Virginia Reed's pony and wanted to trade for it. Her father refused, in no uncertain terms, but they wouldn't take no for an answer and tried to take the pony. Mr. Reed got angry and rode back a mile to speak to their chief, who had promised us safe passage.

The chief, who was dressed most splendidly, came riding up at full gallop on his horse and drove the braves away from the pony. He was so mad he fired arrows at his own men! They gave up on the pony and ran away, and the rest of the braves left us alone.

"We're most fortunate they're busy fighting the Crow, or they might be fighting us," Edward's father pointed out. "They outnumber us ten to one. If they were of a mind to, they could defeat us in less than in an hour."

For days after we left Laramie, the Indians rode among us, always peaceful, and then one morning they were gone, and we ain't seen them since.

✦ ✦ ✦

July 8

The passage of our wagons has been slow, more like a snail than a train, and a lot of the folks have been complaining. Some of the bachelors, the men who ain't got families to care for, have left their wagons behind and gone ahead on mule or horseback. They can make thirty to fifty miles a day that way. Meantime we keep slogging along, getting no more than fifteen miles on our best day. That's barely more than a mile's progress each hour. Why, a baby can walk faster! For that matter a full-grown man can *crawl* faster. But what are we to do? We could travel much faster without the wagons, but the families need all the belongings they carry in the wagons, if they are to start a new life once we reach our destination.

Yesterday we unloaded a piano and left it by the side of the trail. The man who owned it was intending to teach music, but he said the coyotes were welcome to play that d—mn piano now, as his oxen were too tired to pull it any farther. We could hear the wind in the strings for miles after we left it behind.

July 9

It has been powerful hot. Near 100 degrees at noon, even tho we are slowly coming to the higher elevations. That means the livestock must be watered frequent, and that makes us even slower. Then as soon as the sun goes down, it gets so cold we have to wrap ourselves in our new buffalo skin blankets and shiver until dawn.

I keep hoping that once we finally cross the Đivide, it will be downhill all the way to California. I said as much to Edward's father, but he only smiled and shook his head. "Don't work that way. But at least we have plenty of food," he said.

That's true. There are still buffalo to shoot, but we must eat the meat right away, as we have no means to preserve it.

July 12

At present we are in the valley of the Sweetwater River. We are passing through a stark landscape such as few people have ever seen, with high bluffs and rocks that rise like islands from the bare ground. The strange scenery is a welcome change from the endless prairie of weeds and sage, but the going is even more difficult.

Yesterday at noon we passed through the Devil's Gate, which is a gap through the high mountains. It is barely wide enough for two wagons abreast, but the dark granite rises 400 feet or more on either side and blocks out the sun. You can see the light ahead, but while you're in the shadow it's cold enough to chill the blood. Nobody said much. All you could hear was the creaking of the wheels and the grunting of the oxen echoing off the giant slabs of rock.

When we finally got through, I made a joke to Mr. Breen about "leaving the Devil behind," but instead of joking back at me, he got real serious.

"I fear we have not done so," he said, staring straight ahead. "The Devil rides among us."

I asked what he meant, but he wouldn't say no more.

July 14

This may be our lucky day. That's what James Reed said, when we came upon a man on horseback, traveling east. The man was carrying a letter from Mr. Lansford Hastings himself, addressed to any emigrants he might meet along the trail.

In the letter, Hastings says he has discovered a new route to California! If we follow his instructions, we save 350 miles. Think of it, 350 miles! It has taken us nearly a month to travel that distance! Follow Hastings and we shall save ourselves four long, hard weeks on the trail. Follow Hastings and he promises to guide us himself, once we have reached Fort Bridger!

I was so excited by that letter I couldn't help but believe Mr. Hastings, even tho the old mountain man said Hastings was a fool who didn't know anything about guiding wagon trains, even tho he did write a book on the subject.

The only one that spoke up in opposition was Mrs.

Tamsen Donner, who reminded us that the old trail was well known, and that many hundreds have gone before us and been successful. We know nothing of this new trail, she said, or what awaits us there.

Mr. Reed took a deep breath. You could tell he was fighting to control his temper. "I fear we must, madame, for we are far behind schedule. If we do not take Hastings' advice and save ourselves a month of hard travel, that month will come to haunt us."

"What if it is Hastings' advice that comes to haunt us?" Mrs. Donner asked.

Mr. Reed had no answer, except to say that the final decision would not come for another week, when we would come to a fork in the trail, and have to make up our minds which route to take.

July 18

Poisoned water. That's but one of the troubles we've been having on our way west. All day long we fought through the sand, having to drag the wagons out time and again, until we were all so exhausted and thirsty we could hardly move.

Finally we came upon a stagnant pool of water and stopped to let the cattle drink. Right away several got sick, and two of Mr. Donner's oxen died. They lay down on their bellies and moaned and rolled their eyes, and then never got up.

We don't dare drink the water, but must rely on what little we carried, until we clear these badlands. It has put us all in a grim mood and worried about the future. Good water don't seem so important when it's plentiful, but when it's hard to come by, there ain't nothing more valuable.

July 19

Don't matter whether we feel high or low, today was the day we had to make our choices. First choice was who should lead the wagon train. Mr. James Reed made it plain that he believed he should be chosen. He has every confidence in his own ability to lead us, with help from *The Emigrants' Guide*, which he values like the Bible. But Mr. Reed is such a high and mighty man that many in the party do not like him, and so instead we chose Mr. George Donner. He does not have Mr. Reed's experience, but he is solid and friendly.

From now on we are to be called the Donner Party.

On the second choice, Mr. Donner and Mr. Reed are in agreement. We have reached the fork in the trail and must go left to Fort Bridger and to Mr. Hastings, who will guide us through the "cut-off" that will save us weeks of time and get us to our destination sooner. We are all of us in agreement on this choice, except for our new leader's wife, Tamsen Donner, who has been fretting on the decision for a week.

Once again, Mrs. Donner asked if there was no way she could persuade us that now is not the time for experiments. What do we really know of Lansford Hastings? she asked. How do we know he is not some vain adventurer who will lead us into peril, if he leads us anywhere? Hundreds of wagons have taken the right fork and made their way to safety, she said. Why must we be the ones to try a new way?

It was her husband who spoke first, seeking to comfort her. "My dear wife, I more than anyone am aware how this choice has troubled you. I can only say that any wagon train of emigrants must face hard choices as they travel west through lands unknown to them. This is but one more choice, and the majority are in agreement. Give us your trust, my dear, and we will not lead you astray. Every member of this party will arrive safely, that is my pledge."

Mrs. Donner nodded mournfully and said no more.

July 20

For the whole day we broke new trail, and it was hard going. Mr. Donner estimates that Fort Bridger is but a week away, and there we shall find new provisions. There

Mr. Hastings will be waiting to guide us over the "cut-off" he mentioned in his letter and deliver us to California at last.

Tonight we are camped near the Little Sandy River. There are mosquitoes here as big as hummingbirds, and we sit wrapped in our blankets, swatting these giant, bloodthirsty insects and staring at the fire, hoping we all made the right decision.

I am confident we did. Mr. Hastings wouldn't write to us about a new route over the mountains if he didn't know about it, would he?

July 26

At last we have reached Fort Bridger. I told Edward it would be a proper fort with high walls and guard towers, but I am wrong. "Fort Bridger" is nothing but a couple of rough log cabins and a corral for the horses and cattle they are selling. The cabins are owned by trader Jim Bridger, who named it a "fort" after himself.

Edward says if Fort Bridger is a fort, then he can build a lean-to this afternoon and call it Fort Edward, but he is just pulling my leg. Still, he's got a point. You can't judge anything out West by the name. Chimney Rock ain't no chimney, and Fort Bridger ain't no fort.

"I expect you boys are disappointed," Mr. George Donner said to us, "but Mr. Bridger seems to be a good man, and he has what supplies we need—tho his prices seem a trifle high."

A *trifle* high? I heard him charge a man ten dollars in gold for a pint of whiskey. Ten dollars in gold would buy a small saloon in the backwoods of Missouri! And it ain't only the whiskey that costs more. Everything does. Barrels of flour, clothing, patent medicines, oxen—everything costs ten times what it should. Old Jim Bridger is getting rich off the poor emigrants, that's for certain.

Tamsen Donner suspects Bridger is in cahoots with Lansford Hastings, because the shortcut Hastings is promoting goes right by Fort Bridger. The more emigrants come this way, the more money he squeezes out of them.

Me, I don't know what to believe. Just because Bridger charges too much don't mean the shortcut is no good. Edward's paw says you have to expect supplies to cost a lot more when they've been carried out to the middle of nowhere. He says supplies will be expensive in California when we get there, too. The only cheap thing is land itself, and mostly that's given away for nothing if you stake a claim.

It does stick in my craw, tho, Mr. Bridger taking advantage like that.

We expect to camp here for four or five days, resting the oxen and making repairs. Mr. Lansford Hastings, who has promised to meet us here and guide us over his shortcut, left before we arrived and has gone out exploring, gathering material for his next book.

He is a very busy man and promises to make contact with our party at some future date. I ain't holding my breath.

July 28

More Indians passing through. These are not the Sioux braves, but another tribe they call Snake Indians. Mostly they are women and children walking and dragging litters behind them. They are friendly and like to shout "gee haw!" at the oxen, to show they can speak a few words of our language. Mr. Bridger says they are on the move because they want to avoid the Sioux and Crow war parties. He says the Snake People won't fight unless they have to. The way he said it meant he didn't have no respect for the Snake Indians, but why should they fight if they don't have to?

I like the Snake People, they are very polite and respectful and never tried to cheat us. Unlike Mr. Bridger, who looks sly and always has his hand out.

August 2

Poor Edward! We were but a few days from Fort Bridger, traveling alongside the Bear River, when the accident happened. Me and Edward and Virginia Reed were riding out ahead of the wagon train. So far the land is good, with plenty of grass for the cattle and clean water from the river. There are fish in the river, too, and some of the men have caught them.

Anyhow, me and Edward and Virginia were out riding, and Virginia, being the youngest and a girl, got to showing off. She said her pony was faster than Edward's horse, and he said it weren't, and to prove it they raced. It turned out Virginia was right—her pony was the fastest—but before the race was over, Edward's horse tripped and fell, throwing Edward to the ground.

I heard him cry out and went running. Poor Edward was lying on the ground clutching at his knee. His leg was broke bad. Real bad. So bad the bone was sticking out of his shin.

"I done it now," he sobbed. "Paw will kill me, he sees what I done."

I told him to hang on and I would go for help.

Before I left, Virginia came up. The grin on her face sort of froze when she saw what happened. She was real sorry, and said she would stay with Edward while I went for help.

I rode back to the wagon train and shouted out what had happened, and Edward's paw came with a small wagon. Turned out Edward was wrong about his paw being mad. Mr. Breen took one look at the leg and said,

"You are a brave boy for not crying. I hope you will not think less of me if the tears come to my eyes."

With that, Edward let out the tears he'd been holding back, and his father cried, too. When we lifted him into the wagon, he fainted from the pain, which his father said was just as well, as there is only so much pain a body can handle.

At every bump of the wagon poor Edward moaned. He asked would I tell no one about him or his father crying, and I made a solemn promise not to speak of it. I was worried his broken leg was bleeding so much, but there was nothing we could do.

Later

When we got back to the wagon train, folks gathered around and said they'd never seen a leg broke so bad, not since the boy got crushed by the wagon and died. Edward's maw told them to hush up, that this was a different sort of injury and her son would survive, thank you very much.

All the commotion attracted the attention of a mountain man who was heading for Fort Bridger, loaded up with furs. Soon as he heard someone had broke a leg, he made it known he was an expert in fixing busted bones.

"I broke both of my legs and set them myself," he bragged, showing off his skinny, bowed legs.

He was a bit scrawny for a mountain man, but made up for it by being hairy as a bear. I swear, even his ears sprouted hairs thick enough to braid.

Anyhow, once the mountain man heard about poor Edward's misfortune, he wouldn't take no for an answer. "I fixed more fractures than any doctor. Show me to the boy!"

Folk brought him along to the Breen wagon. Edward had already fainted dead away when his paw clicked the bone back in place and bound it with a splint. The mountain man looked down at Edward, and the blood-soaked bandages, and he said, "If that leg don't come off, it will kill him."

Edward's maw moaned and cried out to the Lord.

"The flesh will putrefy, that's a certainty, ma'am."

Mr. Breen asked was he sure, and the mountain man said he had seen legs that weren't broke half that bad that killed their owners. It must come off, and the sooner the better, or it would be the death of him.

Just then Edward's eyelids fluttered. "Maw!" he cried out. "I dreamt they took my leg! Is my leg still there?"

The mountain man went off to get his knife and saw that he kept in a pack on his mule.

Edward then begged that his leg not be cut off. He said it was better already, since his father had set the bone. He offered to swear on a Bible that he wouldn't die, if only they'd let him keep his leg.

The mountain man came back with a piece of folded leather. He unwrapped a small, wicked-looking meat saw and held it up to the light. "Three strokes and it's off. Quick is best, ma'am. Better tie the boy down, so he don't squirm."

Edward then kicked up such a fuss, begging and a-pleading, that his maw and paw finally agreed to put off taking his leg, to see how it might heal.

Finally Mr. Breen had to pay the mountain man five dollars to make him go away, which he did, muttering that Edward's flesh would putrefy, and that he would surely die.

We are all praying that the mountain man is wrong and that Edward's leg will heal.

August 6

Yesterday we crossed a most perilous river. The water was white with foam. We had to unhitch the oxen and take them across, bellowing and fighting us every step of the way. I can't blame the poor critters, as the river frightened all of us. One wrong step and we would be swept into the savage currents and smashed against the boulders.

Mr. Breen shouted that we must keep their heads above water. I promised to try, and did my best. We managed to get most of the oxen over safe (one disappeared into the water and didn't come back up) but then had to work the wagons over by hand, pushing and pulling with all of our strength. I weren't strong enough to make a wagon move, so I stood on the wheel spokes to add my weight and help make them turn.

Edward and his maw were in the wagon, hanging on for their lives. Poor Edward is still hurting bad, tho he says the pain ain't as bad as it was. I could tell he wished he was out with me and the other men, and not having to lay abed at the mercy of others.

He moaned only once, when the wagon struck a boulder sideways. Little damage resulted, and we soon had them safely ashore, and the oxen hitched up again.

"That was fine work you done," Mr. Breen said, thanking me. "We were lucky the day you come along and shared this journey with us."

I had to cough and pretend to fuss with the oxen, so's they wouldn't see my eyes were wet. Because I'm thinking it was me who got lucky when the Breens took me in and treated me like one of their own.

Maw and Paw must be watching over me.

August 7

Stay where you be, and send for me.

That's from the note we found upon entering the canyon. It was left on the limb of a tree for us by Mr. Lansford Hastings, who is out ahead exploring his shortcut and has promised to lead us. No one knows what to make of it, exactly, and many of the women are angry at the men for following Hastings in the first place.

Tamsen Donner pointed out that we never even laid eyes on the man, and yet we are trusting him with our lives as the rumor of him leads us farther and farther into the wilderness.

Her husband has sent Mr. James Reed and two other men ahead to find Hastings and to see why he wants us to wait. Meantime the hours and days are passing, and we ain't getting any closer to California.

August 10

James Reed returned this day. The news is all bad.

Mr. Reed told us how he rode deep into the canyon and soon understood why Hastings had requested that we wait.

We gathered around the fire to hear the news. Mr. Reed didn't mince words. He said it was a nightmare ahead. The way it is strewn with boulders and pits that would swallow a wagon whole. There are more dead ends than you'd find in a maze, and stretches so thick with bushes and cottonwood that we'd be hacking at them until the world ends.

Tamsen Donner stood up and asked the question we were all thinking. Why then did Mr. Hastings send us here? What of his shortcut?

He said on the third day he finally got clear of the canyon and caught up to Mr. Hastings and his party, just south of the Great Salt Lake.

What did he say? we all wanted to know. What did Mr. Hastings have to say about his guidebook to California, and his shortcut?

Mr. Reed at first mumbled, and then had to repeat himself. He said Mr. Hastings sent his regrets.

Edward's paw jumped up from where he'd crouched by the campfire and demanded to know if Hastings would lead us, as he had promised.

You could tell James Reed didn't want to look Patrick Breen in the eye. He didn't want to look anybody in the eye. He said it wasn't likely Lansford Hastings could spare the time to lead our party. It seems that Hastings had bad intelligence about this particular canyon. He had been told it would be clear enough and easy for wagons. Obviously whoever told Mr. Hastings that was mistaken.

Tamsen Donner looked ready to jump up and down, she was so steamed. "What you mean to say is that Mr. Hastings was mistaken, and that we were mistaken to follow his so-called shortcut! A shortcut that obviously does not exist!"

Mr. Reed took that very stiff. He said we should not blame Mr. Hastings. An explorer must rely on intelligence from various sources. Guides and trappers and Indians and so on. They were at fault, not Mr. Hastings.

Another one of the men stood up and said it was obvious that Hastings, the great author and explorer, wasn't man enough to face us. The Hastings' shortcut was a bust.

Mr. Reed was silent for a time and then said whoever was at fault, it was done, and we must find our own way.

The last thing Tamsen Donner did before she went to bed was carry out their copy of *The Emigrants' Guide to Oregon and California* and throw it into the fire. Her husband looked like he had a mind to stop her and then changed his mind. Mrs. Donner didn't say nothing, she just turned away and stormed back to their wagon, while her husband looked most sorrowful and watched the book shrivel up and burn to ash.

I have writ this all down late at night, by the light of a candle, long after the campfires burned down. I have never seen the party so discouraged. The blackness of this canyon has seeped into our hearts and stolen away our hope.

August 11

The canyon is so dark, and the walls so high that only a small strip of stars is visible overhead. It is as if we've fallen to the bottom of the world and can't see our way out.

If we are lost, then how shall we get to California? Somebody suggested to go back on our tracks and return to Fort Bridger. But if we return to Fort Bridger and take the old path, it will be too late. There will not be time enough to cross the mountains before the snow comes. Nor do we know if Mr. Bridger would let all of us abide with him for the winter, as we do not have enough supplies to see us through, and it is unlikely that he would undertake to feed us for all those months.

So there's no point going back. We are doomed if we do and doomed if we don't. That is what the men say, and Mr. Reed did not disagree.

The bad news has hit Mr. Reed very hard, for he feels responsible for promoting the idea of the shortcut. I do not like Mr. Reed much, because of his arrogance, but even I can see that the fault is not his alone. Mr. Donner pushed for the shortcut, and now we must suffer the consequences.

Never has the hour been so dark, or my heart so cold. I can only pray that dawn will bring us new hope, or at least a way out of this terrible canyon.

August 13

Our progress has slowed, so it ain't hardly progress at all.

What happened is Mr. Reed took it upon himself to find a way through the canyons, since Mr. Donner didn't have no ideas on the subject. His wife, Tamsen, is still mad enough to spit about the fix we're in.

Anyhow, Mr. Reed went exploring and found us another canyon that didn't look quite so bad as the first one. Only it turned out worse. We made less than five miles, most of it in the wrong direction, and then discovered we'd have to cut and chop our way through miles of cottonwood that grow so thick a man can't walk through it sideways.

August 14

The women and children stayed in camp today while we cut a narrow road through the canyon. Tomorrow we shall get free and be on our way.

August 15

Today we discovered another blocked-up canyon less than a mile beyond where we cut a narrow path. So we are back to cutting and chopping. The men are trying not to act discouraged in front of the women, as everybody is very frustrated. No one talks much about it, but we're all afraid we'll be trapped in these canyons until winter comes.

August 17

At last we cut our way out of the canyons and came to a gap in the mountains, but we had to cut through that, too. Mr. Reed named it "Reed's Gap" after himself. He can have it. We had to hack our way through a thicket of green willows, and every time I swung my ax I thought how mad I was at Mr. James Reed for acting so high and mighty, and for causing all this trouble just because he was too bullheaded to admit a mistake.

Had we taken the old and proven path that a thousand wagons have taken before us, we'd have made 100 miles by now. Instead we're fighting willow thickets and cottonwood tangles and giant mosquitoes and flies that bite like rabid dogs. We're working from dawn till dusk, until we drop from exhaustion. So hard we can't see straight and can barely talk.

I don't mind the sweating or the bug bites or how tired it all makes me, what scares me—what scares us all—is the time we're losing. I never thought much about time or what it means, but time is everything when you got to get over the high mountains before winter.

Already the nights are very cold, and some folks claim they can smell snow coming. I said there ain't no way snow can stick in August, and they reminded me that we're almost halfway done with August, and that winter comes very early in the high elevations. They say there ain't no autumn season in the Sierra Nevadas, it goes from summer to winter overnight.

✦ ✦ ✦

into pulling, shouting "Haw! Haw! Move you stubborn, stupid ox, move! Haw! Haw!"

August 25

Luke Halloran died this day of consumption. We paused to bury him and then got back to work.

August 26

In the end it took much, much longer to pull the wagons over the mountain one by one than it would have to cut our way through the canyon. Seems like every decision we make is the wrong one and costs us time.

Tonight Virginia Reed asked why did I look so glum. Her daddy says we have but a short way to the Great Salt Lake and the grass is good for the cattle.

I mumbled something about being tired, but it isn't getting to the lake I'm worried about. It's getting to California. It seems like the more we go forward, the farther away it gets. Like we're chasing a bright cloud that keeps slipping over the horizon.

It has taken us eighteen days to go forty miles. A man on horseback can do that in a day. I have a horse of my own, and could leave the party and make my way alone, as others have. I'm a good hunter and could trust to finding game. But even thinking such thoughts makes me blush with guilt, because the Breens have been so kind to me. How could I abandon them now? Leave my friend Edward with his broken leg? Leave his maw and paw to fend with the others?

Only a coward would act so, and I am no coward. Even if I am afraid.

August 27

We came at last to the Great Salt Lake with little difficulty, having finally crossed the Wasatch Mountains that gave us so much trouble, with all the dead-end canyons.

The Great Salt Lake is shallow and so salty it can't be drunk. No one lives there, not even Indians, but near the southern part there are springs not yet contaminated with salt, and we were able to water the cattle, and ourselves.

"We have but one long day's drive across the salt desert, and then we shall be in good shape," said Mr. Reed, standing high upon his wagon so he could be heard by all. "I expect we shall be in California within a month, surely by the end of September. Indeed, I feel confident that I may promise safe arrival by then, if not sooner."

Nobody said nothing when Mr. Reed finished his speech. We've heard him talk that way so many times it don't mean nothing.

August 28

Today we found a ragged note from the cursed Mr. Hastings, tacked on a board set in the crook of a tree. The note had been torn to bits by birds. Some of us thought being torn to pieces was the right fate for anything connected with the so-called explorer, but Tamsen Donner took it upon herself to piece the note together, in case it might contain some crucial information.

It took a while but when she finally got the note put back together it was more bad news.

"'Two days, two nights. Hard driving. Cross desert. Reach water,'" she read, with her voice shaking, and then whispered, "Lord help us."

"Two days and two nights hard driving." We all know what that means. The way across the salt marsh is much longer than we anticipated. Cattle can't go more than one day without water, so what are we to do?

Can we carry enough to get us there? Nobody knows, not even Mr. Reed, who says he knows everything. All we can do is go forward and trust to Providence. But so far, Providence ain't been good to us. We fear the oxen may die before we get to water, and us with them.

In a few minutes I will lay me down to sleep. Maybe things will look better in the daylight.

August 30

At last, night has come, and the cursed sun is finally gone from the burning sky.

So far we been two days and nights crossing the salt desert and can't see the end of it yet. No water anywhere. Not even dew drops. The salt sucks up every drop. If a man is foolish enough to waste water by spitting, the spit disappears the instant it hits the ground. No water but what we brought along, and there ain't near enough of that.

We must keep moving. If we stop, we die, that is the law of nature.

✦ ✦ ✦

August 31

Another hard day.

The salt flats are hard and white and dead flat, and go out as far as a man can see. They might go on forever, for all I know. Seems like it, most times. Nothing grows here, not even a cactus, because the earth is poisoned with salt. You can smell the salt in the dust, and it makes you thirsty. You can feel the salt parching your mouth, your nose, your lungs. My skin is so dry it feels like the paper I'm writing on.

The poor oxen, with their noses in the white dust, cry out for water most piteously, but the water must be rationed. All we can do is soak rags in a bit of water and lay the rags against the oxen's tongues. It seems to give them some comfort.

At the height of noon the sun sits on top of your head and burns through your skull, into your brain. A sun so bright it's hard to see. I keep my kerchief partway over my eyes, and the brim of my hat down, and still it shines so hard it hurts, and makes your eyes dry and itchy.

The light plays tricks, too. The heat comes off the salt flat so thick it makes the air woozy, and everything blurs. The wagons are strung out, with the lighter wagons miles ahead, and sometimes the distant oxen look like giant creatures—like elephants, or something even bigger and older than elephants.

Far over the horizon you'll see a magical mountain

kingdom floating above the world. Then you blink and the magical mountains are gone, and there's nothing but the palest blue sky and the blinding sun, and the white, white nothing of the salt flats.

Some folks think they've seen the Pacific Ocean floating in the sky. They say they seen the waves breaking, white with foam, and that California beckons us, that we shall cleanse ourselves in the sea, and drink from the springs of Eden.

Thirst is making them crazy. Thirst is making them see things that only exist inside their sunburned heads. Although, truth be told, today I saw another wagon train, identical to ours, some miles away across the salt flats. The heat tricked my eyes into thinking the wagons looked much larger than ours, and the people were ten feet tall or more, a race of giants! But when I raised my hand to wave, one of the giants waved back, exactly as I did.

It was a kind of strange, mirrorlike mirage. There was no other wagon train, only us, and we saw ourselves reflected in the heat.

✦ ✦ ✦

September 2

It is night. We are still crossing the salt desert. We been rationing ourselves to just a swallow of water every two hours, and at night the swallow stays with you for a while. The cattle complain less, too. They are all 'round better natured than most of the people.

This evening, just before sunset, one of the men came to the Breen wagon, believing that the Breens have water to spare and are hoarding it for themselves. He had his kerchief up over his face, but we recognized him from one of the straggling wagons, some miles behind. He had come up on foot and would not be turned away.

"I must have water," he gasped. "Gimme a gallon or two, I know you got plenty!"

Mr. Breen looked around like it was a cruel joke. Where would he keep plenty of water? "You are mistaken, sir," he said, and suggested the man return to his own wagon.

With that the fella pulled out a pistol and waved it in Mr. Breen's face and said he must give him some water or he'd put a bullet in Breen's head. So Mr. Breen gave the man a jug of water, and he vanished into the night.

My guess is he drunk the stolen water himself, long before he got back to his wagon or his family. Out here in the desert, when thirst drives a man crazy, water is like whiskey. It makes you do things you'd never think of doing, if you wasn't so mad for it.

One thing is for sure. We're no longer a party of

emigrants, helping one another along the way. It is every family for itself. Mr. James Reed may have the biggest wagon and the most cattle, but he and his wagons and his family are falling farther and farther behind, and no one is much inclined to help, even if they could.

September 4

We saw James Reed come riding by on his best horse some hours ago. Said his oxen had been unhitched from the wagons and were being driven ahead to find water. Meantime he bragged how he'd ride to the end of the desert and bring water back to his family. That is his plan.

Once he'd gone riding off like a man leading a cavalry charge, Mr. Been turned to Mrs. Breen and said, "How'd you like it if I left you stranded in the desert to go off on an adventure? Would you like that much?"

Mrs. Breen shook her head and said she felt sorry for poor little Virginia because she believes her father can do no wrong. And so far he has done nothing right.

Mrs. Breen is right to say "poor Virginia." It's not her fault her father is bullheaded, and took us so far from the regular path, and lost us in the canyons.

At the same time I'm not so sure James Reed is doing the wrong thing, riding ahead to find water. What else can a man do, if his family is dying of thirst? Do nothing and you die, same as what happens when you stop moving. Maybe he'll find water and maybe he won't, but at least he's trying.

I will stop here. I am too thirsty to write more.

September 5

We are resting at Pilot Springs, having at long last made it across the blasted salt flats with most of our cattle surviving. That is, most of the Breen cattle surviving. Many others had cattle and oxen that perished, or stampeded away as thirst drove them mad, and have been lost in the desert.

All but a few of the wagons had to be abandoned in the desert, too. Whole families walked the last twenty or thirty miles on foot, at night, with nary a drop to drink.

Mr. Donner said we must rest here at the springs for several more days, and go back at night to recover the abandoned wagons, one by one. All of us will help, whether the wagons belong to us or not. I think we are all ashamed of how so many of us acted when death stalked us on the cruel salt flats and want to make up for it by acting neighborly.

Edward is now nearly able to walk, and talks of nothing but joining me again on our adventures. His maw and paw are content and grateful for having survived the ordeal of the salty desert.

The Reeds have not fared nearly so well. All of their

wagons were finally abandoned, including their greatest pride, the grand Pioneer Palace Car. It seems that James Reed finally made it back to his family, but with only just enough water for them, and not for his cattle or oxen. So he and his wife and children had to walk the last thirty miles on foot, at night, in a howling windstorm. Meantime all his cattle got loose or stampeded and are gone. He blames the men he hired to drive the cattle, for giving up and thinking of themselves, but no one else blames them.

Let him rant and rave about lazy fools and cowards. It will do him no good, for overnight the Reed family went from rich to poor, as most of their fortune was tied up in cattle and wagons. He has no one to blame but himself, and yet he blames everybody but himself. He vows he will return to the salt flats and recover his wagons.

September 6

You got to hand it to James Reed. The man don't give up. He went out onto the flats with one ox, hoping to find his missing cattle. All but one of the cattle were gone, but he somehow managed to get the Pioneer Palace Car back to the camp. His other two wagons he had to leave in the desert. His daughter, Virginia, was overjoyed to see their main wagon again, as most of her belongings were in it.

"Oh, Father!" she cried out. "You have done it! You have done it!"

Mr. Breen heard her, and muttered, "Oh, he done it all right. He has taken us halfway to Hell. Most likely he'll take us all the way, if he gets a chance."

Then Mrs. Breen told him to hush up, and he did.

September 10

Finally we left Pilot Springs and continued on our long journey, but not before trouble found us yet again.

When I first got up this morning, shaking and shivering with the cold, Edward cried out, "Look! Snow!" And sure enough, the hilltops were dusted white, tho none of it touched us down here. It looked fresh and clean, but it sent a chill through my bones.

Many of the smaller children laughed to see snow so early. The children don't know enough to be afraid. The rest of us took a mournful aspect because we know that snow means winter, and winter comes early in the high mountains. We got to get through the high mountains or perish. Snow is our enemy.

Time is our enemy, too. Mr. Donner figures we got three weeks to make up for lost time, and if we don't, we will be lost, too.

Before we left the springs, the men took inventory of our supplies. No surprise, we ain't got near enough provisions. So we took a vote to send a couple of men ahead to Captain Sutter's Fort, in California, as fast as they can. Charles Stanton and William McCutchen were chosen. They will go on muleback—much faster than by wagon—and if they make it, will explain to Captain Sutter that our party is in a bad way and needs help.

George Donner asked me if I wanted to go with them and take my chances, but I will not leave so easy. I have cast my lot with the party, for good or bad.

"I thought you'd say that," said Mr. Donner. "Good. The Breens need you, and the party needs you, too. You are a fine shot and a hard worker. I must hope that your loyalty will be repaid with kindness and with good fortune."

I told him I was sure it would, but that was a lie. I ain't sure of anything, except I never felt so lonesome in the midst of so many people. They say we are closer to California than to Missouri, but it seems like our destination keeps getting farther away. The harder things get, the more I dream of my old home, and the less I dream of California. I suspect there are others who feel the same way, but no one speaks of it. Talk of home is forbidden—we must only think of our destination.

Anyhow, I watched the two men ride off until they disappeared over the horizon. We don't know if they'll be able to get supplies at Sutter's Fort, or if we'll ever see them again.

Mr. Donner says they are good men, but what does being good have to do with it? About now I'd rather be lucky than good.

We covered more than twenty miles today. That's good. The bad part is, we have hundreds more to cover.

More oxen died. So we ate them.

September 13

Much fighting today. It ain't the Indians we are fighting, but one another. It started with the women. Some of them got together over the morning campfire and started complaining about the men, and all the stupid things we done, like taking Mr. Hastings' shortcut.

"Hastings' Shortcut!" one of the women crowed. "Two words and both of them a lie! Hastings is a liar, and there ain't no shortcut! We should be over the mountains by now and instead we are still on the plains, with hundreds of miles yet to go! All because the men believed a liar!"

Mr. Reed took exception and defended himself. He said he understood they were all disappointed in our progress thus far. "But we all voted to take the shortcut," he said, "and must live with the consequences."

"Voted!" the woman shrieked. "It was only the men who voted! But it won't only be the men who die! No, sir, women and children will die, too, if something isn't done! It was you got us into this! You and the other men! All so you could have an adventure and pretend to be explorers. You forgot our purpose!"

James Reed had his hands on his hips, and he wouldn't back down. His eyes looked like chips in a cold fire. He asked what they thought their purpose was.

The women said it was to get their families to California the best and safest way possible. And that he had failed, and that we should already be there but we were not.

Mr. Reed didn't have a reply. He grunted and strode away, and later I heard him complaining to his wife about the ungrateful people, and how if he'd been elected leader of the expedition instead of George Donner, things would be different.

The fighting didn't stop when Mr. Reed backed down. Soon the women were fighting among themselves, and insulting one another's husbands. Many of them were so angry they cried tears of rage.

I kept to myself. I am a man but can't argue with the women, for they are right. It was pure folly to follow Mr. Hastings' suggestions. But the mistake happened weeks ago, so what good does it do to chew it over now?

Mr. Breen whispered to his wife that there must be bad air from the sulfur springs that makes people so angry. Maybe so. But the women didn't say anything that wasn't true. We are in a bad way. We have barely enough oxen left to haul the wagons. There is some bacon left, and barrels of flour, but not near enough to last all the way to our destination.

We know our situation is grim, but we keep moving. We keep going. What else can we do?

September 20

We are camped this night in the Ruby Valley. It is cold enough that my breath comes out like fog and my fingertips tingle with the cold. I ain't bothered writing in this journal lately because each day brings more discouragement, and writing about it makes me weary.

Shoshone Indians have sneaked into the camp at night and stolen two of Mr. Reed's horses. He says he will kill the horse thieves if he catches them, but Mr. Patrick Breen said he wouldn't know a horse thief from the wrong end of a horse, and Mr. Reed took offense and retired to his wagon.

There has been much unpleasantness between the people. Nobody shares the campfires no more. Each family sticks to itself, and fends for itself. We ain't no longer a party together, but only a cluster of wagons traveling in the same direction. Bust an axle and you are on your own, or dependent on a few friends.

I asked Mr. Donner if there was something could be done, but he sighed and shook his head. "We are in a bad patch," he said. "Maybe things will improve, once we get over these mountains."

He means the Ruby Mountains, which surround us on all sides. Seems like we been among these mountains forever, and have made little progress west. We been following a wagon trail, the mark of emigrants that have gone before us. Emigrants that are far ahead of us, likely because they never took no shortcut.

One good thing, there are many fresh springs, and plenty of water, and enough grass to keep the cattle alive. Edward says the worst is over, and from here on it'll all be downhill. I didn't have the heart to tell him we got many more mountains to cross, and higher ones, too. He's in a fine mood because his leg has stopped hurting. Seems like a million years ago he broke it and the mountain man wanted to cut it off, but it was only six weeks ago. Six of the longest weeks that ever a man has lived.

Another good thing happened. I laid out in the bush for two hours, tracking paw prints, and shot three rabbits. So me and Edward and his family had a good hot meal for supper. Rabbit stew, seasoned with a little salt and pepper.

We didn't share with nobody else, as there wasn't enough to go round.

October 6

A terrible thing has happened. A thing so awful I can hardly bring myself to write it down.

Yesterday, after lunch, James Reed killed a man.

It happened like this. The wagons were having a hard time of it getting up a hill, and tempers were short. There were three wagons ahead of Mr. Reed's wagon, and he got impatient and tried to pass one of the other wagons, as his oxen were stronger.

When he came alongside the other wagon, Mr. John Snyder, who was driving, cursed at him and said he was there first and must take his turn.

Mr. Reed took exception to Snyder's language, and Snyder said if Reed didn't get back in line he'd whip him like a dog.

Snyder then showed Reed his whip, which he'd been cracking over the head of his poor oxen.

Reed said only a coward whips dumb animals.

"I'll show you who is a coward!" Snyder roared, and he leaped out of his wagon.

Snyder then scampered up to where Reed was driving his own team of oxen, and struck Reed a blow with the butt end of the whip.

Reed was stunned by the blow, but soon recovered. He shoved Snyder away from the wagon and snatched a hunting knife from his belt. "Keep away from me!" he screamed. "Keep away, or I swear I'll kill you!"

I had never heard Mr. Reed scream. It made him sound young and different, like he wasn't in charge of himself no more. He waved the knife at Snyder, who laughed in his face. Reed started after him, but Mrs. Reed leaped out of the wagon and pulled him away.

Then, as Mrs. Reed tried to lead her husband away, Snyder unfurled his whip and cracked it over their heads, and this time the lash struck Mrs. Reed, who cried out in pain.

I saw the color drain from James Reed's long face. His eyes got big and round, and he ran straight at Snyder with his knife. Twice more Snyder's whip struck him, once on the arm and then again on the head, but it was like Reed couldn't feel nothing but his anger.

Snyder tried to whip him a third time, but by then Reed was upon him and stabbed the knife into Snyder's chest.

Snyder fell down, looking surprised.

Reed threw his knife away and made a high, wailing sound. "What have I done?" he cried. "What have I done?"

Snyder got to his feet and staggered a few paces. He come toward our wagon, holding his hand to his chest. Mr. Breen jumped down to help him, but he couldn't be saved.

After Snyder died, Mr. Reed acted regretful and offered to help bury the man he had killed. He wasn't allowed. The sentiment among the party was that Reed had committed murder.

Lewis Keseberg, who hated Reed ever since Reed

admonished him for beating his wife, saw his chance for revenge. He said it wasn't fair for a knife to go up against a whip, and that Mr. Reed had committed murder.

Many others agreed. James Reed had made many enemies with his arrogant ways. Even George Donner did not rush to defend him, but said the matter should be settled in a court of law, once we reached California.

While Snyder was being buried, Virginia Reed helped bind up her parents' wounds. Her mother was bleeding from where Snyder's whip had struck her neck, and her father from the blows upon his head. They both looked very downcast, as if they knew the incident would not end with Snyder's burial.

We banged up a plain coffin for the dead man and set him into a shallow grave. Nobody had much to say on his behalf, as Snyder wasn't no more popular among the party than Reed, on account of his quick temper and his foul mouth.

Edward's paw said a few words over the grave. That was all. There wasn't time for a lot of Bible reading, because the party still had to decide what to do about Reed.

Keseberg made it plain he believed Reed should hang for his crime, the sooner the better.

Mr. Donner said that Reed had gone too far and killed a man out of anger, and that given our situation, we must settle the matter ourselves, rather than waiting for a court. Then he proposed a vote that instead of hanging,

Reed be banished from the wagon train. He asked for a show of hands.

And so we voted to banish James Reed. I blushed when Virginia saw me raise my hand, but I didn't see no other way. If her father stayed with us, the next thing he'd be in a fight with Keseberg, or with somebody else. Some folks were already talking about burning his wagon if he stayed. There weren't no choice about it—he had to go away.

"Run him off!" somebody shouted after the vote was taken, and many of the folks thought he should leave with nothing but the shirt on his back and the boots on his feet.

Mrs. Reed then begged us to let her husband take his horse, his guns, and such supplies as he might need.

In the end, George Donner agreed that Reed should take a horse, but denied him any supplies, as all supplies were needed for the members of the expedition, and for that matter, Reed's own family.

When he left, James Reed sat tall in his saddle and promised his wife and daughter that he would go ahead to California and bring supplies back to the wagon train.

Little Virginia wept most piteously as her father rode off, until her mother shushed her and put her in the wagon.

Later

Tonight after the party had camped and eaten what little we had for supper, I snuck into the Reed wagon and found Virginia still crying.

"Go away, Douglas Deeds," she blubbered, hiding her face in her pillow. "How could you vote against my poor father?"

I explained, the best way I could, that being banished was better than hanging, or having their wagon burned. My heart ached for the heartbroken girl, and I agreed to help her in any way I could.

Before I quite knew what was happening, Virginia took me by the hand and led me out of the back of the wagon, into the darkness. She had bundled up her father's rifle with some powder and shot, and three day's ration of food, and intended to carry it to him.

I didn't really want to help James Reed, but couldn't say no to his daughter. And so we snuck away from the camp and hunted about until I found the marks of his horse. There was just enough moonlight to see the faint trail in the sandy soil.

As we walked along following the hoofprints, Virginia said her father was not a murderer, but only defending her mother.

I did not argue.

We found Mr. Reed no more than a mile from the

camp. He was hiding behind a hill, holding the reins of his horse, and waiting for us in the darkness. I understood then that he had arranged to have Virginia bring out his rifle and the supplies, and had been waiting for us as near to the camp as he dared.

He asked if I would go with him to California and I said no thank you. I didn't say that riding into the night with a known killer wasn't my notion of a good idea.

Just before he left, Reed kissed his daughter on the forehead and made a solemn vow that he would find Virginia and her mother wherever they might be, and save them, and that someday soon they would all live happily together again.

Then he rode off.

Virginia wept quietly all the way back to camp.

I slept that night under the Breen wagon and hoped they'd never find out what I had done. Not even Edward, who is my best friend in the world.

II
Starvation Lake

October 20

It has been two weeks—two very long weeks—since last I wrote in this journal. At times I've been so discouraged it felt like what is the point of writing when all is lost?

I mean, who cares what happened to Douglas Allen Deeds of Independence, Missouri? If he was dumb enough to join up with a wagon train of greenhorns and head out into the wilderness, who wants to read his stupid journal? Probably nobody. But still I feel like I should write things down when I get the chance, if I ain't too exhausted to hold the pen and make my marks.

I say we are "greenhorns" cause that's what they call beginners who don't know nothing, and we didn't know nothing about exploring or crossing the country by wagon, and that's a fact. We didn't have no business going west without an experienced guide. We know it now—even Mr. Donner admits it—but there is nothing to be done except keep moving as long as we can, and hope supplies reach us from Sutter's Fort.

If they don't, I may have to eat this journal, page by page.

October 21

We've been having a load of trouble from the Paiute Indians. The Shoshone tribe pretty much kept to themselves, but the Paiute delight in making us miserable.

Paiute are always ready for war, and if they can't find a war to fight, they raid. Mostly they prey upon our cattle. Those they can't steal, they kill. So far they killed or stole more than forty head, which leaves us barely enough to pull the wagons we got left. There are less wagons, too, as we have had to abandon quite a few along the way, when they got broke or stuck, or didn't have no oxen.

Tamsen Donner says the Paiute are dogging us because we look weak. She says they think we are stragglers who don't know how to find our way, or to fight, and mostly she's right. Expect we do know how to fight, only it's with one another.

For instance, one day Edward's paw, Patrick Breen, got his horse stuck in some bad mud. At the time we was far back from the others. I ran up as fast as I could and begged a man to come back and help us pull the horse out.

The man refused. He said Patrick Breen had hoarded his water when we crossed the salt desert and wasn't deserving of help.

By the time I got back, the horse had died, and I didn't want to tell Mr. Breen what the man said, as it would only cause more trouble.

October 22

Tonight only a few of the wagons camped together, and the Paiute got bold and came up so close we could hear them breathing in the dark. They hooted like owls, just to provoke us, and then laughed when one of us fired off a gun and didn't hit nothing.

All of a sudden we heard this strange whistling noise—you couldn't tell where it came from—and then arrows whizzed out of the dark and stuck in the wagons. Nobody got killed, but I figure if them Indians had wanted to kill us, we'd all be dead by now.

October 23

Some of our trouble is just plain blockheaded stupidity! The men who were supposed to guard the cattle from the Paiute decided to come back into camp and have breakfast, leaving the cattle and oxen unguarded. That's exactly what the Indians were waiting for, and they swooped in and stole or killed about another two dozen head.

All this trouble with the Paiute makes me wish Mr. Reed was still with the party. Maybe he'd know what to do. Certainly he wouldn't allow the horses to be left unguarded.

Of course we don't know if he's alive or dead. But I think he's alive. Say what you like about him, he's a tough buzzard, and if any ignorant tenderfoot can fight his way to Sutter's Fort, all on his own, he can.

Not quite everything was bad today. Before sunset we got our first sight of the Sierra Nevada mountains, away off in the distance. They looked cold and sort of faded blue, and about as far away as the moon.

Then the clouds came down and we couldn't see them no more. I can feel them, tho I can feel those high Sierra mountains, just a-waiting on us. On the other side is our destination. Cross the mountains and we have but sixty miles to go!

I am hopeful once more, if we can only get to the mountains before the snow falls.

◆ ◆ ◆

October 24

My old horse, Barny, died this day. He was a good horse, and I will miss him terrible.

October 25

Today is a great day! Help has finally arrived! Charles Stanton has found us, and he carries food and supplies for our bedraggled party. Stanton was sent off on a mule six weeks ago, with instructions to find his way to Sutter's Fort. By the grace of God he did so, and Captain Sutter in his great generosity gave him fresh packmules and supplies to bring back to us. Flour, jerked beef, beans, and such. Glorious, most glorious!

At first we thought he was a mirage made by our desperate situation. We had just begun our assault on the Sierras and were faint of heart, for the peaks are higher than the clouds themselves. It seemed impossible that any man might find his way across such an imposing mountain range, let alone a party that included women and children.

Then Edward, who had been alongside the oxen, caught sight of something. He jumped up on the wagon and shaded his eyes, looking off in the distance.

"Men," he said. "Three men and seven mules!"

That was enough to make us hurry forward, driving the mules up the slope, to make our rendezvous with the miraculous mirage.

But it weren't no mirage, it was Mr. Stanton and two Miwok Indians who were hired to guide him. At first we was all so stunned we could scarcely speak. And then everybody started talking all at once, and it took a while to sort things out. Stanton told us he'd had many hardships, and would have perished were it not for his Indian friends, who are called Luis and Salvador.

Then Stanton dropped a stunner. He told us that James Reed sent his regards. He said Reed had also reached Fort Sutter and was now mounting a proper rescue party, with more supplies than Stanton could carry.

Except by his family, James Reed hadn't been missed. Now, however, in light of our situation, we were all prepared to accept him as a hero again, if he should manage to rescue us.

Virginia and her mother wept to hear the news. The rest of us were too busy making up biscuits from the flour and frying them in the bacon grease that Stanton gave us. He only carried enough food for six days or so, but it is enough to give us hope, and to admire his courage for risking his life to find us.

The real miracle is that he has been over the Sierras to California and back. If he has done it, maybe we can, too. Mr. Donner pointed out that we have come near two thousand miles since we started this trek. Sixty more miles will get us there.

That's all, just sixty miles. Surely we can make

sixty miles in six days? That is only ten miles a day. Walk a mile an hour for ten hours, and we shall easily make ten miles a day!

Can we take this as a sign from Heaven that our prayers have been answered? Can we?

November 4

This day has broke my heart.

Yesterday, after a brave and ceaseless struggle up the steep and perilous trail into the high mountains, with Stanton and his Indians to guide us, we came at last to the final pass. The trail was so narrow we had to leave the wagons behind and carry our things on our backs. Set a foot wrong and you'd slide all the way back, or worse, slip over the edge of a cliff and fall to the bottom of the world.

It was late in the day, and everyone was very discouraged. There was a foot or more of snow on the ground, and some drifts much higher, which made for hard going. To make it worse we could barely see. The wind blew from the west, fierce and cold and wet with freezing rain.

Then one of the packhorses slid into a gully and was nearly killed, so we stopped and couldn't seem to get going again.

I have never in my life been so cold and miserable and tired.

When Stanton saw the state we were in, he advised that we rest until dawn and then work our way through that gap. He tried to sound lighthearted, for our sakes, but there weren't nothing lighthearted about the cold and the dark and the howling wind.

Luis and Salvador, the Indian guides, didn't complain about the miserable weather. They just wrapped themselves up in their blankets and stood under a tree, as if they'd been planted there. Pretty soon the snow dusted their blankets so that they almost looked like trees themselves. Once in a while they'd shake off the snow, but other than that, they never moved.

The rest of us gathered around a small fire of pinewood and tried to keep warm the best we could. Nothing worked. It was like you could sit right in the fire and the wind would steal the hot away.

Nobody said much. We all knew this was our last chance, and that we must seize it and trust to Providence. Already Stanton's supplies have run out, and we are dependent on what little we've hoarded. Our wagons are left behind, or taken apart, and we have only what we can carry on our backs. Our prospects could not be more dire, if we do not get over the mountain soon.

Stanton remained calm. He puffed on his pipe and said, "Pray for deliverance, my friends. Pray for the sun to shine, and the snow to melt."

November 5

Our prayers, alas, were not answered.

All night the wind shrieked, and the rain turned to icy pellets of snow. The flames of the fire soon faded and died. No one could manage to strike a spark and relight the fire, the wind was that mean. Ice formed on the dead white logs, and the cold settled into our bones, as if our own fires had gone out, too. The night lasted forever, it seemed like, we did not even know for sure when dawn came.

Later, with a little light in the sky, Stanton and the two Indians went forward to see what the night had left us. I followed behind them, slogging through knee-deep snow. My feet were so cold I couldn't feel nothing from the knees down. We come around a stone outcropping, the pass or gap that led down to the other side of the mountain, and that's when the full force of the storm hit.

In an instant, the air was white and thick with the storm. Snow pellets smacked into us like a hail of frozen bullets. Stanton tied a rope to his Indian guides, and they went down into the gap, to see if it was passable.

They didn't get far. The snow was ten feet deep, and they sunk up to their necks, and had to dig their way back out. I helped as best I could, and me and the Indians managed to drag Stanton back behind the rock, where the wind wasn't quite so bad.

It took Mr. Stanton some time to get his breath back. His throat was partly froze by the snow he'd swallowed, and it was hard to hear what he said.

"Retreat," he croaked. "Must retreat."

And so we have retreated a few miles, and found shelter near a frozen lake. Shelter from the wind, but not from the snow, that continues to pile up, covering everything in a thick, frozen blanket until it looks like the mountains were carved of ice, instead of stone.

Mr. Stanton, who is usually cheerful and confident, was crushed by the turn of events. He said had we got here two days sooner the pass would have been clear, and all would be well.

But two days are gone, and we cannot have them back. Winter has come and will not let us go. We are trapped in the Sierra Nevadas, only sixty miles from civilization, but it might as well be ten thousand.

November 6

The Breens and I were lucky. We've found refuge in a deserted cabin that may have been built some years ago by a fur trapper. The cabin is very crude—felled logs with no windows, and roofed with pine branches. There are holes in the roof. The stove is broke, but it is a great improvement on being outside. Outside where the storm rages and the wind screams through the mountaintops and over the lake. Outside where the last few cattle are dying almost without complaint, as if grateful the end is near.

Soon we will eat the frozen cattle, and scrape what little meat we can from their skinny bones. And then, when that is gone, what shall we eat?

Shall we eat the snow? Shall we eat the ice? Shall we eat the bark on the frozen trees?

What shall we eat?

November 10

We are still alive, but prospects are grim and getting worse.

After the pass got snowed in, we had two more storms, and the wall of snow that blocks our way is now twice a man's height, with drifts even higher. We are no longer a party, but the survivors of a failed expedition. We've split up, more or less, and must live on our own. Or die on our own, if it comes to that.

November 11

There are twelve people abiding in the Breen cabin, including me. The dirt floor got slick and muddy once we got a fire going, and warmed up considerable. Since we moved in, Keseberg and his family have built a lean-to against the side of our cabin. The Murphys, the Graves, and the Reeds have all built themselves shacks not far from us, and shelter inside them the best they can. Nobody visits that much. All the families keep to themselves and eat what they have managed to hoard or hunt.

It has snowed most of five days steady. The snow gets deeper every hour that passes.

The Breens are better off than most. Patrick Breen had six head of cattle, and we soon slaughtered them. The meat and bones were then stacked and hidden in the snow, where they have froze up hard and won't go bad.

Mr. Breen thinks he may have enough meat to keep his family alive for the whole winter, if need be—and if he don't have to share it out with others less fortunate. Share with them and his own family would likely starve.

He didn't say so, but I knew he meant a time may come when I am not welcome at his table. Were he forced to choose between his family and me, the family must be chosen.

I'm not angry, as it is only natural to protect your own, and I am grateful for any kindness they may give me. For the time being, Mrs. Breen sees I get a little beef to chew upon, and I have kept up my strength.

November 14

Edward looks at me with sorrowful eyes, as if he suspects that one day I will be banished from the family cabin and will be his friend no more.

I told him not to worry, that soon an expedition would arrive to rescue us.

I wished I believed it was true, but how can anyone think to rescue us with all this snow? You can't walk through snow so deep. It's like trying to swim in thick water.

We got word the Donners have made camp a few miles away, nearby the creek. They are in bad shape, as the snow killed most of their cattle, and they have very little to eat.

Mr. Stanton came by in a rage, as Indians slipped into the camp last night and stole three of his mules, that he was hoping to take down the mountain when the weather cleared. He is very vexed because the mules was loaned out by Captain Sutter, and Stanton feels he must return them.

I asked why the Indians who stole the mules didn't help us, as they must be aware we are slowly starving. Stanton pulled a little on his pipe and said it was because other settlers and trappers have shot and killed some of their people. White men treat them like animals. So they take their revenge by stealing.

Poor Mr. Stanton, who was brave enough to set out

trying to rescue folks he didn't even know, is trapped like the rest!

Something must be done, he said, and we must do it, because no one can mount a rescue party under these conditions. I asked what could we do, and he said he didn't know yet, but he was thinking on it.

Charles Stanton has very little food of his own, but must rely on portions from those who do. So far folks have been generous, as they can't forget it was Stanton who risked his life to bring us supplies, and they are still grateful to him.

That may change as supplies dwindle. Hungry folk ain't likely to share when all they can think about is their own hunger and staying alive.

✦ ✦ ✦

November 22

Yesterday I joined Charles Stanton and some others, as we attempted to get through the pass and down the mountain on our own, with some help from Stanton's remaining packmules.

The attempt began with high hopes, on a fine, sunny day. It had not snowed for most of a week, and enough of the snow had melted for us to get through the pass without too much difficulty. Partly this was the crust of ice on top of the snow that lets us walk above it. The poor mules, being heavier, were not so fortunate, and had to struggle through six feet of thick, heavy snow.

Our little expedition was led by Stanton's Indian guides, Luis and Salvador. They ain't from a mountain people but know more than white men do about trekking through deep snow. I think they are fine fellows, but some of the others grumbled that we shouldn't put our lives at risk on the word of no Indians.

Wasn't it Indians who killed or stole so many of our cattle and horses?

Mr. Stanton said he trusted Luis and Salvador as much as he trusted any white man and made it clear he didn't want to hear no more complaints about our guides, and from then on it was only whispers. You can't stop a whisper. It always finds a way to fly from ear to ear.

Our progress west was good, once we got through the

pass, and by nightfall we were several miles down the mountain. We'd have made it even farther than we did except for the mules. We had to keep stopping and waiting for the mules to catch up, and by the end of the day the poor critters were exhausted with their efforts.

November 23

Last night, as we sat warming our hands and feet around our little campfire, Mr. William Eddy allowed as how we should abandon the mules. He said dragging them along slows us down, and suggested we leave them behind and race to the bottom of the mountain while the weather was still fair. He said this crust of ice was a blessing. A man can almost run across it, and that with conditions like this we can make Sutter's Fort in two or three days.

Stanton heard him out and then shook his head and said he could not leave the mules, as they were not his to abandon.

Mr. Eddy insisted and said surely Captain Sutter would understand that a man's life was worth more than a few mules.

But Stanton refused and said he gave Sutter his oath he would return his property. We could do as we liked, but he must return to the lake and wait for a better chance.

Many of the men argued with Stanton for hours.

Finally they threatened to go ahead without him, using his Indian guides. But Luis and Salvador were loyal to Stanton and would not leave without him saying so, which he would not.

In the end, Stanton won the argument by being as stubborn as the mules. The mules wouldn't budge, and Stanton wouldn't budge.

Finally we gave up. Took us all of one day and most of one night to get Stanton and the mules back to the camp on the other side of the pass. By then we was all spittin' mad, and terrible disappointed that our expedition had been a failure.

November 25

Too late.

Some of us younger men was about to mount another expedition through the pass when a storm hit us bad. The icy crust that made walking easy has been buried under another foot of snow, and more of it piles up every hour.

Stanton has seven mules left but they are in poor health, with their ribs showing.

I did a terrible thing today. I prayed the mules would die soon, so that Stanton and the Indian guides would feel free to lead us down the mountain to Sutter's Fort.

December 1

The great storm is over.

The steady snowfall worked itself up into a blizzard that blew most fearsome for two days and two nights. The shrieking of the wind was so loud we couldn't hear ourselves talk. The wind sounded like the mountains screaming. Finally we quit trying to talk and huddled closer and closer. The stove in the Breen cabin only gave out a little heat because the wood was almost gone, and no more could be found with the storm raging.

I tried going out for wood but didn't get five feet. The wind wanted to tear me apart and bury me. I gave up and barely made it back to the cabin. They said I was a fool to try, and that I could have been lost in the storm, and they were right on both counts.

Patrick Breen said we must wait it out, that no storm lasts forever. Maybe not, but it sure seemed like forever. Then when the wind finally stopped screaming, we went out to find we had been blanketed with six feet of fresh snow.

Worse, the remaining cattle and Stanton's mules are nowhere to be seen. Either they were driven off the mountain by the wind, or the Indians used the storm as cover and come by to steal them away. Either way it don't matter: The critters are gone, which makes it all the more useless that Mr. Stanton wouldn't leave them behind when we had the chance.

He came by the Breen cabin after the storm and all but

apologized. He said he regretted that he could not fore-see the future, and that had he known the mules were doomed, his decision would have been otherwise.

For some reason that made me laugh. "Heck, if I could see the future, I wouldn't be here at all," I said. "I'da never left Missouri in the first place."

Stanton nodded. He didn't seem quite so low as I expected, considering, and soon enough I found out why. He said he had a new plan, and that some of the peo-ple were going to make "snowshoes" and walk out. Was I interested in coming along?

I asked what were snowshoes, and he said they were an Indian invention. With snowshoes it seems you can walk on top of the snow, according to Luis and Salvador.

It sounded like a crazy idea, but what have we got to lose? I told Stanton I was his man, and would help make snowshoes if somebody showed me how.

I figure if Jesus could walk upon the water, then maybe we could walk upon the snow, if we prayed hard enough.

I'm praying hard.

✦ ✦ ✦

December 8

Clear weather today, but the snowshoes still ain't ready. Charles Stanton and William Eddy are making the shoes out of oxbows. First they have to split the oxbows into thin frames, then bind 'em together and weave rawhide across the frame.

They are making twenty pairs and it seems like it's taking forever. Partly this is because both Stanton and Eddy are weak from hunger. Stanton has to leave off working on the snowshoes to beg for food, but he don't get much.

Even Patrick Breen, who is normally a kind man, won't let me share with Mr. Stanton. What little they give me is out of my friendship with their son, Edward, Mr. Breen reminded me. He said Stanton is a good man but must fend for himself.

December 9

There is nothing to eat but frozen pieces of lean and stringy beef that Mr. Breen thaws out on the stove. No flour, no bread, no salt, no vegetables. I keep dreaming of turnips swimming in salty butter, and potatoes, and green peas, and sweet corn, but all I get is a few ounces of gray beef that tastes like soggy bits of leather. It's enough to keep you alive, but you still feel weak all the time, and your stomach is always begging for more, and making sure you never forget how hungry you are.

It must be much worse for Mr. Stanton, tho he makes no complaint. Neither do the Indian guides, Luis and Salvador, who are just as starved as he is. All of them are getting so thin the wind blows through them.

It ain't fair, but I can't seem to make it right. I went out today looking for game to give to Stanton and the Indians, but didn't find none. I had hoped to find a squirrel out of his nest, or a bird lighting on a branch, but there ain't much game this high up the mountain, and what there was of it got shot in the first few days. Going was hard, as the snow came up to my chest. It is like swimming against the current in a frozen river.

I am eager to try the new shoes that promise to float on top of the snow, and would do it while the weather is still good.

December 10

Word came up from the Donners, who are still camped with a few other stragglers down by the creek. They say the Donner family is in much worse shape than the rest of us. They lost most of their cattle in the first storm, and have taken to eating mice, and chewing on buffalo hides.

I feel bad for Tamsen Donner, who was right to worry about taking the shortcut. She knew the thing to do was stick to the trail but couldn't make the men agree with her. Now she must nurse her poor husband, who is very ill, and take care of her young children as best she can.

When I told Edward how unfair it was, that good people should starve because they made a mistake, he said we were in God's hands, and if God wanted us to live, he would provide food. I said I hoped he was right, but just in case God left us to fend for ourselves, I aimed to leave with Mr. Stanton's expedition, whenever the snowshoes were ready.

Edward thought it a bad idea to leave the warmth of the cabin and take my chance in the open air. He urged me to remain with the family and said he would see his paw gave me enough to live.

Edward is my friend and thinks of me as a brother. But his paw don't think like that. I can tell by the looks he gives me that he'd as soon have me leave and save that much more meat to keep his own family alive.

I try not to take it personal, but sometimes it feels like no one can see me but Edward, and maybe his maw. The others tend to look right through me like I wasn't even there. It don't matter that I could have left them months ago but stayed to help. All that matters is what happens right now.

It seems that hunger makes a man forget his thankfulness.

December 11

Snow and rain. Firewood is getting very hard to find, and we must huddle around a cold stove. Miserable weather!

December 13

More snow. Everyone short-tempered and quick to take offense. I fear it will never end, and that we will be trapped until hunger kills us, or we kill one another.

Mrs. Reed gave Stanton a little dried meat for our journey. She is the only one who remembered his previous kindness.

December 14

More snow and freezing rain. Snowshoes ready when the weather improves. It must improve, it must!

December 15

We are ready at last.

III
The Forlorn Hope

December 17

The sun finally came out this morning as we made our escape from Starvation Lake. There are seventeen of us using the snowshoes. They really do make it possible to walk on top of the snow, once you get used to it.

Charles Stanton and the Indians will guide us. He says there is an outpost forty miles to the west and believes we can get that far in four or five days, if the weather holds.

We carry very little with us. A small portion of tobacco and some dried meat and coffee, enough to last four days if we're careful and don't give in to our hunger. It is important to travel light and move fast, and besides, that's all the food that could be spared for us.

We call ourselves the Forlorn Hope. Our little party includes ten men, two boys, and five women.

When we came up to the pass and saw the mountain peaks marching higher than the clouds, and how far away the valley looked below, Mr. Stanton raised his walking stick and said, "Look about you! We are as close to Heaven as we can get!"

Then the wind came up and took the words from his mouth. Like the mountains were laughing at us for trying to escape.

It was hard going, but we got through the pass okay.

Then, like they say, it was all downhill—only downhill is a lot harder than you might think, unless you done it on snowshoes. We knew about the cold and the wind and the snow, but the sun was a surprise. Here we been praying for clear weather, and now that we got it, the sun wants to burn us blind. It comes off the snow something fierce, like a cold flame that burns through your eyeballs and fries the back of your brain.

I got a scrap of cloth over my eyes that helps a little. It's much worse than the blinding glare in the salt desert, because everything is covered with snow, and snow is brighter than salt. Somebody said it was like lying in a white mirror at high noon and freezing, all at the same time.

We ain't traveling together, exactly. We're stretched out, with the fastest in front and the slowest bringing up the rear. Following along in one another's snowshoe tracks. I expected the women to be the slowest, but they are not, not by a long shot.

The slowest, big surprise, is Mr. Stanton, who was supposed to lead us.

The thing about snowshoes, you got to run sort of bowlegged, and it wears you out. Plus we're already weak from not eating right. Poor Mr. Stanton had trouble keeping up and kept falling behind.

The first time it happened, I went back to help him. He was slumped against a tree, catching his breath, and waved me off.

He told us to go on, that we mustn't slow down for one man. He said our purpose was to reach civilization and send a rescue expedition back to save the others. If we wait for him, we would put all of them in peril.

It still don't seem right, but I did like he told and went on my way. I got so far ahead I couldn't see him when I looked back, and that fretted me constant, almost as much as being so hungry all the time.

We made about six miles downhill before night fell.

Stanton finally caught up about an hour after we'd already stopped and built a fire. And when he did come straggling in, he just sat down and didn't have nothing much to say, like the words would cost him too much energy. Turned out that even when the sky got dark he was still mostly blinded from the glare off the snow all day, and the campfire hurt to look at.

"See to yourselves," he muttered, and would say no more.

"We did good today," said William Eddy, nodding to each of us. "Tomorrow we will do better."

We will sleep crouched by the fire, as close as we dare, and hope the sky stays clear, even if that means suffering from snow blindness. Better snow blindness than snow blizzards!

I am dog tired and can't write no more.

December 18

Two of our party gave up this morning and returned to Starvation Lake, as they are too weak and hungry to continue.

We bid them luck, and farewell, and promised to send a rescue team back for them, when we have reached civilization. Then we picked up our packs and tightened our snowshoes, and moved on, traveling west. Always traveling west, with the cruel sun to guide us.

I'm much worried about Mr. Stanton. He can't keep up with the rest but lags far behind. None of us dare slow down for stragglers. We are running for our lives, and must make the outpost before a blizzard buries us or the wind turns us to ice.

Flurries came up in the afternoon, and the sky turned a mean shade of gray. Nobody will talk about it, but we all feel a big storm coming.

December 20

This night we stopped and made a fire, but Mr. Stanton never did catch up.

Earlier this morning, as we gathered our packs to leave the campfire behind and hurry on our way, Stanton remained by the smoldering fire, puffing calmly upon his pipe.

When Mary Graves, who is one of the strongest of the Forlorn Hope, told him we must leave, Stanton said he would be along soon. But he didn't move from his log by the fire.

I noticed his eyes never went to Mary when she spoke to him. So I shuffled over, careful to keep my snowshoes out of the fire, and crouched beside him and asked was he blind.

He did not look at me, but told me again not to worry. He said I had miles to travel and mustn't fall behind.

I told him he had been a great inspiration to us all and then took hold of his arm and tried to raise him up. Gently he removed my helping hand. "Thank you, Douglas. Go on. I'll follow soon. I promise. Let me rest a little more, and then I'll be on my way."

Some of the others shouted at me to get moving, or be forever left behind.

I knew they were right, and that I must keep moving or die, but I never felt so wretched as when I left Charles Stanton sitting by the fire, smoking on his pipe like he didn't have a care in the world. Like he was finally at peace and didn't want to be disturbed.

The going was very hard this day. Not only because poor Stanton made my heart so heavy, but because the wind began to howl through the trees. We walk upon ten or twelve feet of snow, and at any moment the wind can lift a foot of it and fling it in your face.

And the cold. I've come to hate the cold like I'd hate my worst enemy. The cold goes through your bones and makes you weep, and then the tears freeze and you're still so hungry it hurts inside, and crying don't help, it only makes you weaker.

The Forlorn Hope didn't make but four miles today, struggling for every inch. By now we should be well below the snow line, on solid ground, but we ain't. The snow is so deep we walk among the tops of trees. Maybe the snow goes on forever, no matter how low you get. It sure looks that way.

Nobody said much as we built our fire and sat close with our blankets joined, holding in the heat. But we was all thinking about Mr. Stanton, and hoping he would come stumbling into camp like he did before.

We sat together for two hours, our stomachs rumbling something awful, before William Eddy suggested we share out our last ration of dried beef.

"What about Mr. Stanton?" I asked. "We'll put aside his ration, right? For when he catches up?"

Mary Graves sighed and said she saw no point in saving out his portion. She said the poor man was gone and would need no more of our precious food.

I then went over to Luis and Salvador, the Indian guides who had traveled so far with Mr. Stanton, and at such risk to themselves. "Does he live?" I asked them. "Is there hope?"

Luis looked at Salvador, real sorrowful. Then they both looked at me and shook their heads. So we divided up the rations without accounting for Mr. Stanton, and nobody spoke no more about it.

I must write this here, in case I die, and won't be alive to tell the world: Charles Stanton is a hero. It don't matter that he was stubborn about the mules, or if he couldn't keep up because he's been hungry for so long, longer than the rest that wouldn't share with him. He is the only hero among us.

December 21

Bad storm, can't write.

December 22

Yesterday, in the midst of a terrible blizzard, we got a small surprise that pleased us.

Fourteen survivors of the Forlorn Hope gathered in a tight circle around a small fire. The fire kept going out because the snow was coming down so heavy. Each time it went out a pang of cold would shiver up our bones, and make our bodies cry out for food. But there was nothing to eat, as we had consumed all our rations.

Patrick Dolan said he felt more dead than alive, and wasn't sure he could tell the difference no more.

Jay Fosdick agreed, and said we had nothing to fear, because it couldn't get any worse than what we had already endured.

Many of the group then confessed they felt on the verge of death, and that if we weren't delivered of our suffering, they would just as soon join Mr. Stanton in eternity.

Then William Eddy spoke up. He was a good friend of Mr. Stanton and as close to being a chosen leader as we've got. He said Charles would be greatly disappointed to hear such mournful talk and then begged me to try some of my driest tinder and see could I find another spark for the fire.

I did as he asked, and sure enough, the tinder caught and soon we had another fire going, and our spirits raised some. That's when a small miracle happened. William Eddy went into his pack, to read the loving note his wife had left him, and found behind it a small package wrapped in oil skin.

Inside the package was a small chunk of dried bear meat his wife had saved out for him, for a time when he would need it, and think how much she loved him.

Eddy wept like a child, he missed his wife so, and then he shared out the meat with all of us. He could have hoarded it for himself, but he is a good man, and he gave us each an equal portion, exactly the same as he kept for himself.

Cold, dried bear meat. Back in Missouri I wouldn't touch bear meat. Turned up my nose at it. Said I'd rather eat dirt. But out here in the miserable wilderness, with the blizzard screaming through the trees, I chewed it down most heartily. Like it was the juiciest steak in the world, with potatoes and gravy and pie for dessert.

God bless Mr. Eddy for his kindness, and his generosity. He saves us this night, and staved off the Grim Reaper for another day.

December 23

More snow, can't move. Hungry again.

December 24

Tonight, in the icy rain, we miserable few are huddled together and cannot move.

This morning the sky broke clear for a few hours and we were able to make three miles west, with the greatest of difficulty, because the snow drifts were so high and light that even our snowshoes sunk deep with every step.

A little while before noon the weather changed. We are far enough down the mountain so it came in the form of rain. Hard cold rain. Rain that don't have the look of stopping anytime soon. Rain so hard and steady no fire can be lit. The rain soaked into us worse than the snow, sucking away our strength, and left us stumbling around so weak and pitiful it was hard to talk.

It was Mr. Eddy that saved us. He had a plan. He said he'd heard of a thing the trappers do when they get caught in a storm with no fire. It is called the Warming Circle, and we must try it or die of exposure.

At first nobody would listen to him. It's like we was so numbed with the cold and wet he couldn't make us see the sense of his plan. Warming Circle? Blankets? Snow? It didn't mean nothing.

Finally Mr. Eddy grabbed me by the collar and forced me

to listen. The rain was running down his beard and freezing on the end, so he looked like a talking icicle. I thought that was funny and started to laugh until he slapped me.

"Douglas Deeds! Listen to me, please! Help me get the others together!"

That slap in the face brought me back to where I was. Outdoors in the freezing rain, hungry and cold to the bone, and about ten minutes from being frozen to death.

Following Mr. Eddy's instructions, I helped him get us all in a circle. He said he would be the last man in the circle, as things had to be done outside of it first. He made us sit in a tight circle and hold our blankets up to the rain, with our feet all together in the middle. Then he piled snow up around the back of us, to hold the outside edge of the blankets down, and keep the wind from getting under.

The last thing Mr. Eddy did was jump into the middle of the circle and close up the top with his own blanket.

The rain froze on the top of the blankets, freezing them all together. Then snow fell and sealed up the blankets even more. Like making a tent when you ain't got no tent.

After a while, no more than an hour, we began to get a little warmth inside, from our own breath. Soon it was warm enough that many of us began to shiver, where before we'd been so close to frozen we couldn't even shiver, and shivering helped warm us up some more.

Thus we passed the night.

December 25

Raining hard again. We ain't moved in twenty-four hours but remained huddled and frozen together, half buried in the snow. Can it really be Christmas? I think so but am not sure.

All I want for Christmas is not to die.

December 26

I got my wish and am still alive.

Three of the Forlorn Hope were not so fortunate, but went to the Lord yesterday, in the middle of the night, as we huddled together under our blankets, alone in our misery.

Patrick Dolan was the first to go. He had been babbling words that made no sense, as if speaking to invisible people. Laughing and giggling to himself like he was a child again. Suddenly he lurched to his feet, sang a few words from a song, cried out "Mother, I see you!" and collapsed. He didn't move for a long time, and then after a while we realized he would never move again.

Mr. Eddy said the poor man had been driven mad by starvation and it killed him. Nobody spoke no more about his madness, because we were half dead ourselves, and nearly as crazed with hunger as Patrick Dolan.

I asked should we bury him.

William Foster said the ground was frozen. He sounded

angry, as if he wanted to strike someone but didn't have the strength.

I said we could bury him in the snow.

Mr. Foster said, "Leave him be! He might yet prove useful."

Foster then looked around at the others. Several of them nodded, as if in agreement about something that couldn't be discussed. I asked what he meant. How could a dead man be useful? He told me to shut up and mind my own business.

Mr. Eddy made peace by leading us in prayer, and we prayed for the salvation of Patrick Dolan's soul.

Soon after we finished praying, two more died. They just stopped breathing and froze up, and it was some time before we realized they were gone.

Foster looked around at the survivors and said that soon all of us would perish, unless we took advantage of what had been provided.

I was so tired that my poor brain could not attach a meaning to his words. What did he mean, *take advantage of what has been provided*? I meant to ask him, but did not have the strength to speak.

December 27

Last night I dreamt I was lost in a strange country and did not know how to get back home. I heard voices but could not understand. Then I smelled the sweet scent of baking bread and followed the smell, but never could I find where the bread was made, and the not knowing and the not eating made me so dizzy I fell into a blinding white light.

When I woke up, my stomach hurt so from being empty that I had to cover my mouth to keep from screaming.

It was daylight, and the rain had stopped. The other survivors were awake and had thrown off their blankets and were moving around, shivering and talking among themselves in low voices.

I asked what was happening, and what they were talking about, but they all ignored me.

Foster's eyes were glowing strangely. He said we must build a fire and then we would eat.

I cried out and got shakily to my feet and asked what there was to eat.

Foster stared at me so hard it felt like a punch from his fist. Then, speaking very slowly, as if to a child, he said, "We will eat what has been provided."

I asked again what he meant, but he would not answer.

Then I watched as Harriet Pike began screaming about our salvation and then tore apart her coat. At first I thought she had gone mad like poor Patrick Dolan, but she had a purpose. Her coat was stuffed with cotton, and in the deepest layer she found a handful that was dry enough to take a spark.

When she held up the dry bit of cotton, the others

shouted as if she had discovered gold. In a way, the dry cotton was as good as gold, because it meant a fire could be lit. There was no dry wood, so someone suggested a pine tree be set afire, right where it stood rooted in the ground.

It seemed an act of madness to me, that a whole tree be burned where it stood. We had an ax, why not chop it down? But the Forlorn Hope would not wait, and soon the tree was ablaze.

It was a wild thing, to see a group of ragged, half-frozen men and women gathered around a blazing tree, rubbing their hands in the warmth of the flames, their eyes shining with the mad light of starvation.

My whole body screamed for food, but the horror of what they were about to do made me run away from the burning tree, and from the people there. I ran into the woods, atop the snow, with tears freezing in my eyes.

I ran away out of fear that if I stayed, I, too, would become an eater of the dead.

Later

Mr. Eddy found me in the woods, sobbing and crying out that the Lord should deliver me. Like me, he had refused to eat. Luis and Salvador had refused, also, and had gone off by themselves so they would not have to watch the others fill their bellies.

He said we must keep our strength for as long as we could, and he gave me a small strip of rawhide from his snow-shoe. He said I should chew upon it to dull the hunger pangs.

I asked him how the Forlorn Hope could do such a terrible thing. He said they could not help themselves. Hunger makes us animals, and animals do what they can to stay alive.

I moaned that I would rather die than participate.

Mr. Eddy looked at me with sorrowful eyes and said I might feel differently after starving for a few more days.

I pray he is wrong, and that I will not do as the others have done.

December 28

Hid in the woods most of this day, but finally returned when I saw the survivors had built another fire. Could not feel my feet or hands. Huddled by the fire with steam rising from my blanket, but couldn't get warm, no matter how close I got to the flames.

The others looked at me with contempt, as if it is me who had done wrong, and not them. I had not the strength to argue with them. I don't feel angry about what they did. I don't feel nothing much at all. Like my insides were as froze up as my hands and feet.

My hand moves across this page, but I can't feel the words. I am numb to everything, even the prospect of dying.

The strange thing is, I'm no longer hungry. It's like my stomach gave up telling me to eat. All I feel is cold inside my bones, and so tired I can't stand to be awake.

I will sleep now and dream of hot bread, fresh from the oven.

December 29

Too weak to write.

December 30

For three days we remained in the same place, close to the burned pine tree, while the others built another fire and fed on forbidden meat and gathered their strength for the long journey ahead.

I did not eat, but saw their hungry eyes upon me. I decided I must use the last of my strength to walk as far into the woods as I could, so they would not find me when I died.

There was a terrible silence in the woods. The ice on the trees made it look like the forest was made of white bones. I wasn't much better than a skeleton myself.

Finally I came to a tree that had been blown down by the storm. It was a huge tree, and the upturned roots gave me shelter from the wind.

I crouched there and looked up at the sky and thought how beautiful the world was and how sorry I was to leave it.

Strangely enough, I was not afraid. It does not hurt to perish so. Just sit still and the cold will make you warm. You will never have to move again, or feel hungry.

I thought of my maw and paw and hoped they would be pleased to see me.

That's when I saw the rabbit. It had come out of a burrow under the tree roots. It was a big, plump rabbit, fattened up for winter. It looked right at me but was not afraid. Probably I did not look alive enough to frighten it.

I knew then the rabbit was a miracle, and that I must seize my chance or die.

Mr. Eddy said starvation makes a man into an animal, and he was right. Like an animal I grabbed the rabbit and killed it. Like an animal I ate it.

And like an animal I did not think to share with the others.

December 31

I returned to the Forlorn Hope with my strength renewed. No one asked where I had been or what I had been doing.

I did not ask them, either.

We all have our secrets. Mine is the rabbit. I have hidden the leftover meat in my pack, and eat when the others can't see.

❖ ❖ ❖

January 3, 1847

Luis had been guiding us these last few days, through canyons so deep they block out the sky, but today admitted he was lost and had no landmarks to go by, as the snow was too deep, and had buried all the places he knew.

Foster cursed him, and asked what was he good for if he couldn't find his way out of the woods?

That made poor Luis afraid for his life. He and Salvador quietly limped away from the Forlorn Hope. They soon blended into the trees and were gone.

I asked Foster how he could be so cruel, but he would not answer. Then I asked Mr. Eddy what he thought and he said it was better not to think. Just walk, he said. We must keep walking, as salvation may be over that hill.

But there is nothing over that hill, or the next. Or the next. We wander in a world of snow, circling back upon our own tracks, as if trapped in a nightmare that keeps repeating.

I have forgotten what it is to be dry and warm, or to have a roof over my head. I have forgotten what it is to see a person smile, or to smile back, and feel the spirit of human kindness.

What have we become? I cannot see myself—and for this I am grateful—but the other survivors look more like cadavers than human beings.

We are sacks of bones, and the wind blows through us. We are skulls, marching in circles in the wilderness.

We try to keep walking, because salvation may be over the next hill. We try not to think, because if we think too much we'll scream, and keep on screaming.

Later

This is the last of my ink, so these shall be the last few lines I write.

I don't know if I will survive this terrible ordeal. Salvation may be over the next hill, or it may not. But one thing I know. Some folks will do terrible things to stay alive.

EPILOGUE

Bear Valley, California

On the seventeenth day of January, in the year 1847, a young woman named Harriet Ritchie heard a knock upon the door of her small cabin, situated on the edge of the wilderness, within sight of the Sierra Nevada mountains.

The knock was so feeble she thought at first she'd imagined it and went about her business. After a few minutes there was another knock, fainter than the first. Curiosity aroused, Ms. Ritchie unlatched the door and swung it wide.

What she saw startled her so badly that at first she could not speak, and then was moved to tears. Standing in snow up to its bony knees was the skeletal ghost of a young man.

It was only when he moaned that Harriet realized the human skeleton was actually still alive.

"Bread," the ghost whispered. "Bread."

Douglas A. Deeds, a fifteen-year-old from Independence, Missouri, was one of eight survivors of the Forlorn Hope. Weeping at his pitiful state, Ms. Ritchie fed the boy a hot buttered biscuit and then put him to bed.

Young Mr. Deeds recovered his health and briefly

took up dairy farming, as his father had done before him. However, less than a year later he formed a partnership with his friend, Edward Breen, to survey land in the vicinity of Sutter's Fort.

It was to be a lucrative arrangement. By sheer luck, Douglas Deeds and Edward Breen were among the first to discover gold in the most famous gold rush in American history. Both men prospered, settled down, had large families, and rarely talked of the ordeal at Starvation Lake, or among the Forlorn Hope.

Deeds has numerous descendants who still live in the lush and beautiful Sacramento Valley.

Life in America
in 1846

Historical Note

✦ ✦ ✦

Go West, young man!
—John Soule

All hope abandon, ye who enter here!
—Dante Alighieri

In the year 1846 an invention called the sewing machine had just been patented. Ether was first used to dull the pain of surgery. Edgar Allan Poe, the famous author of "The Raven," was publishing horrific stories about being buried alive. Telegraph lines were being strung as the first means of "instant" communication.

The idea of America itself was about to undergo a great transformation. Although its area was already vast, the new nation had a rapidly growing population of twenty million, almost four million of them slaves or indentured servants. Many forces, including the rapid industrialization of the cities and offers of free land, would soon uproot thousands of citizens and send them westward, looking for a new life, and a chance at prosperity.

Just the year before, a new idea had taken root in the American consciousness. As eager American settlers poured into the Mexican territory of Texas, editor John L. O'Sullivan wrote that "it is our manifest destiny to over-spread the continent allotted by Providence for the free development of our yearly multiplying millions." The pop-ulace was soon persuaded that it was America's "manifest destiny" not only to inhabit Texas, but to fill up the entire continent, from the Pacific Ocean to the Atlantic shore.

Mexico had claims on Texas, New Mexico, and California, but had failed to establish any large settle-ments there. In the months prior to the departure of the Donner Party, President James K. Polk annexed Texas and declared war on Mexico, with the intention of gain-ing new territory. Promoters like Lansford Hastings were confident that all of North America would soon be in friendly hands, and sure enough, by July 1846, the fer-tile new territory of California came under American control.

The controversial military triumph over Mexico not-withstanding, America needed to populate California if it wanted to keep it. Potential emigrants were told they would have access to tracts of free acreage, and that the land itself was more fertile and much richer than any previously settled. Books and newspaper accounts made California sound like a veritable Garden of Eden—as indeed it would prove for the luckiest of the settlers. The idea of "going west to get ahead" took on a religious intensity, and even those who were very well established were tempted by the dream of starting a new life in a new land.

And all of this was before anyone even suspected that the hills and riverbeds of California were strewn with nuggets of gold!

When the survivors of the Forlorn Hope finally stumbled out of the mountains looking more dead than alive, that nation was stunned by the tragedy. Within days, rescue expeditions were dispatched, intent on reaching the marooned Donner Party with the greatest haste. Salvation would not come easily. The weather was so bad that winter—the worst in memory—that the first rescuers very nearly died of starvation themselves. It was not until almost a month later, on the nineteenth day of February, that a rescue party finally reached the encampment.

The scene of horror there was almost beyond comprehension. Human bones littered the landscape. Like the Forlorn Hope, those who stayed behind finally resorted to cannibalism. Of the eighty or so emigrants trapped at what would come to be known as Donner Lake, nearly thirty perished. Most were consumed by the survivors.

It took three rescue attempts to save the wretched survivors. James Reed led one of the rescue missions, fulfilling his promise to return. William Foster led another, although he arrived too late to save some of his family members. Conditions were extremely bad, and many of the early attempts failed. With only mules and horses for transportation, and winter storms that continued to rage, it was not until April that the last of the doomed Donner Party were finally brought out.

Among the survivors were all the members of both the Breen and Reed families. The Donners themselves fared much worse. Years later Lewis Keseberg, notorious throughout the West as "Keseberg the Cannibal," never denied consuming the frozen body of Tamsen Donner, the noble lady who had foreseen the horror and been unable to prevent it. It was reported that he often rocked upon his porch, muttering about those he had eaten.

No one in the Donner Party was ever prosecuted for cannibalism, but the horror of what they had done was never forgotten.

The unfortunate members of the Donner Party were not the only eager emigrants who departed from the major jumping-off point of Independence, Missouri, that year. Nor were they any less well-equipped or more badly led than many of the other wagon trains, almost all of which arrived safely.

In the end it was a combination of bad directions, bad timing, and bad weather that doomed the Donner Party to an ordeal of starvation that served as a ghoulish warning to the thousands of settlers who followed in their path—including a little known religious sect that would settle and thrive in the forbidding region of the Great Salt Lake Desert, and become known as the Mormons.

Written by Lansford Warren Hastings (below), The Emigrants' Guide to Oregon and California *provided many people with the incentive they needed to head West in search of a gentler climate and lucrative business ventures. However, the inexperience that informed Hastings' guide would prove disastrous to the people in the Donner Party expedition, who made the mistake of trusting their fate to that little book.*

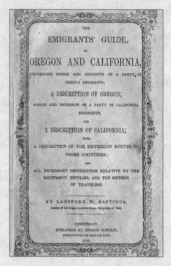

THE

EMIGRANTS' GUIDE,

TO

OREGON AND CALIFORNIA,

CONTAINING SCENES AND INCIDENTS OF A PARTY OF
OREGON EMIGRANTS;

A DESCRIPTION OF OREGON;

SCENES AND INCIDENTS OF A PARTY OF CALIFORNIA
EMIGRANTS,

AND

A DESCRIPTION OF CALIFORNIA;

WITH

A DESCRIPTION OF THE DIFFERENT ROUTES TO
THOSE COUNTRIES;

AND

ALL NECESSARY INFORMATION RELATIVE TO THE
EQUIPMENT SUPPLIES, AND THE METHOD
OF TRAVELING.

BY LANSFORD W. HASTINGS,
Leader of the Oregon and California Emigrants of 1842.

CINCINNATI:
PUBLISHED BY GEORGE CONCLIN,
STEREOTYPED BY SHEPARD & CO.
1845.

Inspired by the promise of fortune and fame in the West, Lansford Hastings wrote his infamous guide in the hopes that hordes of people would follow him and his shortcut to California. While Hastings was indeed a visionary, an experienced traveler he was not. He had never traveled his route with a wagon train, so he could never know the challenges those parties would face.

While each family had at least one wagon, some families, like the wealthy Reeds, had several. And few were as luxurious as the Reeds' Pioneer Palace Car, which housed them along the journey. It had built-in beds and bench seats, and it even had a second-story loft where the children slept.

The Donners and the Reeds employed young men to do the work of driving the oxen on their wagon train. But every person had chores to do each day. Women cooked, cleaned, sewed, and tended to the children while the men cared for the animals, maintained the wagons, and hunted for food.

THE BREEN FAMILY

The Breens were an excellent addition to the expedition as they were farmers and could also read and write. Patrick Breen added music to the bonfire gatherings each night as he played his violin. Pictured here is the entire Breen family. In the center (top) is Isabella, who was the last living survivor of the Donner Party.

Although Patrick Breen's diary contains mostly notes about weather conditions and accounts of the days, it is evident here that the situation of the party was worsening. He writes ". . . it snowed faster last night & today than it has done this winter & still Continues without an intermission . . . Murphys folks and Keysburgs say they cant eat hides. I wish we had enough of them . . ."

141

There came a moment on this expedition that would haunt its members until the end. When they had the choice to follow the path they had planned or to head for the alleged shortcut otherwise known as the Hastings Cutoff, they took a vote and unfortunately chose the latter.

Although Charles Stanton became a hero when he returned, as promised, to the expedition with bread, fruit, and meat, he died peacefully by the fire along the trail of the Forlorn Hope.

Hastings had promised the Donner Party that he would meet them at Fort Bridger to guide them personally, but he never did arrive. And, while supplies at Fort Bridger were excessively expensive, they had no choice but to purchase them there—the next supplier was more than 600 miles away.

The conditions for the expedition were difficult at best. Getting across the Platte River was risky and trying. When the water was too deep, the oxen had to be pulled through and the wagons had to be floated across on rafts.

The treacherous Sierra Pass proved to be a defining moment in a string of terrible luck for the Donner Party. When they couldn't get over it before the first snow, they knew their defeat was inevitable.

It took four separate rescue teams to save the Donner Party. The rescuers employed the use of snowshoes to get them to their destination. Once they got across the frozen, snow-covered lake, they were stunned by the appearance of the survivors, who were desperate and delirious from starvation.

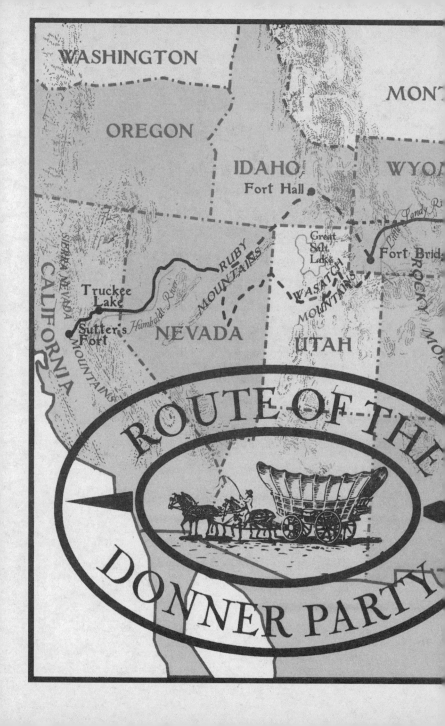

About the Author

✦ ✦ ✦

Rodman Philbrick says, "One of the books that made a big impression on me as a young reader was *Boone Island* by Kenneth Roberts. It tells the true tale of several men shipwrecked on an island within sight of the coast of Maine. The winter weather was bitter cold, they had little hope of being rescued, and at the point of death the survivors finally resorted to cannibalism. Partly the story fascinated me because on a clear day I could just make out the Boone Island lighthouse from the house where I grew up. I could imagine what it must have been like, to be starving and freezing, all within sight of home. The story of what happened to the people of the Donner Party is, I think, similarly horrifying and yet fascinating. To me it symbolized all the excitement and danger of the Western migration. I'm sure I'm not the only reader who wonders what I might do, faced with a similar dilemma in an extreme situation. Of course, I'd rather starve than eat liver, or soft-boiled eggs!

Rodman Philbrick is the author of a number of books for young readers, including *Freak the Mighty*, *The Big*

Dark, Wildfire, Wild River, and *The Mostly True Adventures of Homer P. Figg,* which won a Newbery Honor in 2010. A stage adaptation debuted at the Kennedy Center in Washington, DC, in 2012.

Acknowledgments

✦ ✦ ✦

The author would like to thank Jean Feiwel, Amy Griffin, and Beth Levine for encouraging him to write this book, and for their thoughtful editorial guidance about a difficult subject.

Grateful acknowledgment is made by the author for permission to reprint the following:

Page 138 (top): *The Emigrants' Guide to Oregon and California*. Reproduced from the Collection of the Library of Congress.

Page 138 (bottom): Lansford Warren Hastings. Reproduced from the Collection of the Library of Congress.

Page 139 (top): A Pioneer Palace Car. Courtesy of North Wind Picture Archives.

Page 139 (bottom): Wagon train. Painting by William Henry Jackson. Courtesy of Scotts Bluff National Monument.

Page 140: The Breen family. Courtesy of the Bancroft Library, University of California, Berkeley, California.

Page 141: Patrick Breen's Diary. Courtesy of the Bancroft Library.

Page 142 (top): The parting of the ways. Courtesy of the Wyoming Division of Cultural Resources.

Page 142 (bottom): Charles Stanton. Courtesy of the Bancroft Library.

Page 143 (top): Fort Bridger. Courtesy of Dover Books.

Page 143 (bottom): Fording the Platte River. Courtesy of Corbis-Bettman.

Page 144: The Sierra Pass. Courtesy of the California State Library photograph collection.

Page 145: Rescue Team. Courtesy of the Bancroft Library.

More award-winning novels from Newbery Honor autho

RODMAN PHILBRICK

STAY ALIVE